The Bond

H.L JONES

I would like to say a huge thank you to my family and friends who believed in me and helped me make this come alive. A special thank you to my sister Brittany, if not for you, I never would have started this journey in the first place.

A special thank you to my amazing mentors that helped me through every part of my story's development.

THE BOND

THE BOND

H.L JONES

Contents

I

Yellow Eyes

Flashes of bright colors ricochet around the room, blues and purples collide, the clink, as weapons clash, and bodies intertwine in the heat of battle.

Hate burning all around me, I can't control my body, I'm face to face with a man in his early thirties, tall, with short, shaggy black hair.

Our swords are crossed, and I'm holding him back with everything I have. I can feel his strength as his well-built body bears down on me. My hands are starting to shake under the strain, his deep blue eyes staring at me with a burning hatred.

"I vow I'll destroy everything you love for what you did!" he snarls.

I get a boost of strength, fury burning in me, and I start pushing him. A fire is set inside me now.
"What I have done!" I bellow in a familiar voice, but not my own.

"Your side started all this!" he snaps venomously.

"I want her back! And I'll go through every one of you if I have to!"
I yell back.

My phone buzzes on the bathroom countertop. I shake my head bringing myself back to reality. What was that? It felt so real. My heart is racing, and my hands are shaking as I pick up my phone. It's a text from my sister Mia.

Mia: *We are here, can't wait to see you. X*

I flick a quick text back.

Bree: *Just finished taking a shower I'll be there soon, can't wait to see you, too. X*

I feel awake and refreshed from my morning shower. My heart is still pounding. I wish I could blame my morning fitness class, but I know it's because of what just happened.

I look in the mirror and inspect my reflection. My long, dark, brown hair is doing what I tell it to for a change, and is sitting nicely. My waves cascade over my shoulders and down my back. I notice my eyes are a brighter lavender than usual.

The new black top I just got hugs my hourglass curves nicely, and the jeans I selected are a snug fit. I put my phone, keys, and card into my pocket and sit on the bed. As I start putting on my brown boots, my phone buzzes in my pocket. It's Mia again.

Mia: *Hurry up I know snails that move faster than you! It's a nice day and you are getting out of that damn apartment! RIGHT NOW!*

I roll my eyes, exasperated, as I read her message.

Bree: *Yes mum.*

Mia: *Don't give me that, I'm not letting you bail on us again!*

Bree: *I'm not bailing, I was showering! Sheesh! I'm leaving now.*

Mia: *Good, now move it before I come to get you myself!*

I shake my head, smiling as I slide my phone back into the pocket of my jeans. I finish putting on my boots, and rush out the door to meet her, as I'm not inclined to let her grill me anymore on my time management.

We have arranged to meet in the park today, so my niece Mira and nephew Chris can play, and Mia and I can catch up. I haven't seen her much these days since I quit my P.A job due to.... Let's just say, unappreciated attention. If it wasn't for Tom being in the right place at the right time, I don't want to think about what could have happened.

That happened two months ago, and now I'm not sure what I want to do. Mia has been my best supporter ever since I can remember. That's not saying much, since I don't remember anything from before I was twelve, but she is my world. If it wasn't for her, I don't believe I would have any reason to stay here.

It does not take me long to get to the park from my house, and it's close to the beach. I can hear the waves crashing against the rocks and smell the salt in the air as the light breeze ruffles through my hair. The sun is warm and pricks at my shoulders.

The park is full of swings, slides, sand, and other things to play with, and around the park are beautiful white blossom trees that line the paths, and surrounding areas. It is my favorite place to come in spring.

I see Mira and Chris playing chasey. Chris is darting in and out of the play equipment, trying to get away from Mira, who is close on his tail.

Over on a close-by bench, I see Mia and her husband Tom. These two have been married for fifteen years. They met just after high school and have been glued to each other's faces ever since......No really, I mean it. After all these years, they still cannot leave each other alone for very long.

Tom is sweet, caring, and an amazing husband and dad. He always makes room for me, too. We have a cheeky big brother, little sister relationship.

Tom is a graphics designer and works at a big gaming company. Mia is an English teacher at Chris and Mira's primary school. They are so perfect for one another, anyone can tell how much they love each other still after all this time. I smile at the thought.

Mia sees me and excitement shoots across her face. She jumps up, abandoning Tom to throw herself at me, trapping me in a hug so tight that she lifts me off my feet slightly. I'm sure I felt something crack.

"I'm so glad you're here!" she practically squeals at me.

"Well, I didn't think I would hear the end of it if I didn't," I say back.

"Well, since you quit your job you have been moping around that apartment and that's not healthy. You need to get out and about," she says, waving her hands around to the park.

I purse my lips together. "I'm not moping, I attend my fitness classes twice a week," I retort in a sulky tone.

Mira's cries snap our attention away. Instinctively, Mia and I rush over to see what's happened. We separate, and Mia chases off after a runaway Chris, who obviously knows he's in trouble.

I'm sure Mia knows I have Mira. When I get to her, she is rubbing desperately at the sand in her eyes and mouth, no doubt her brother put there. I kneel down to look into her hazel eyes, that are so much like her mother's.

"Oh dear, what are we to do with the two of you?" I say, dusting the sand off her. I look over to find that Mia has caught Chris and is now walking him back. I would assume she's telling him off from the look on his face.

Once her face is cleared of sand, Mira explains, through hiccups and sniffles, how Chris tripped her up and threw a sand ball at her because she tagged him. I giggle at the silliness and think of Mia and I when we were younger.

I'm six years younger than Mia. She was already eighteen when I was twelve, so we never really fought. She was always mothering me, even before our parents disappeared three years ago on a holiday trip to Egypt.

They were very loving parents and Mia was their only child. Not that they didn't try for more, they simply weren't blessed. They said the day Mia found me by the water's edge near an old boathouse was the day their family was completed.

They took me in and loved me as their own, and Mia always treated me as her sister. She loved me then, and I know she loves me now, but I still have this feeling I don't belong here.

Nothing can be found of me, my parents, or where I came from.

Nothing makes sense. A song from long ago, and the face of a small, dark-haired boy pulling my hair are the only memories I have.

I snap back from my thoughts to Mira, who is a lot calmer now, and is enjoying a cuddle from me. I squeeze her slightly.

"Ahh, Aunty Bree you're squishing me!" she giggles.

"HA! I made you laugh." I beam at her, dusting some more sand off her clothes, and make sure she is okay. Mia is back with Chris in hand, who is refusing to look at Mira.

"I'm sorry." he says to Mira, still looking at the sand in a rough, forced tone.

"I think you can do better than that," Mia says, looking down at him, unimpressed.

He looks up at Mira and repeats, softer this time. "I'm sorry for tripping you, throwing sand at you, and making you cry," Chris says earnestly, rubbing at his grey eyes.

Mira beams at him. "I forgive you," she says, happily grabbing his hand, pulling him to a clear spot in the playground.

Mira starts digging a hole in the sand, and soon Chris joins in, both of them laughing and giggling once again.

Mia and I walk over to the bench, where Tom had been watching all the commotion.

"I feel obsolete watching the two of you in action," he laughs, throwing his arms out to rest on top of the bench he's sitting on. "I was afraid I would get in the way." he adds with a chuckle.

"Afraid of us?" I laugh.

"Ahh, yes! My god, nothing scares me more than a woman on a mission, let alone two!" he says with amused laughter.

"We are not that bad," I say incredulously.

Mia steps closer to him, flipping her short, auburn hair out of her face. "Say that again," she says, crossing her arms in mock annoyance.

I hold my hand to my mouth, trying to hold back a chuckle that turns into an all-out laugh as Tom points at Mia and looks at me with a 'see what I mean' grin on his face.

I can't help my smile from broadening. At this point, Mia places her hands on the bench, on either side of Tom's head. Cheekily, she raises her knees to straddle Tom's hips. He looks up at her, happy with his position, as he runs his hands up her legs to her backside.
"Now that you have me, what are you going to do with me?" he asks Mia seductively. "Please, be gentle," he follows in a coy, playful tone.

Mia's smile grows, lowering her head to kiss him. She seductively growls through her teeth, tugging Tom's ash blond hair to meet her.

"I'm going to see if Chris and Mira need help with that hole they're digging in the sand, all this lovey-dovey stuff is making me feel queasy," I say, acting out being sick.

Mia shoots me a smirk and sticks her tongue out at me.

"Real mature, hard to believe your thirty-five," I retort, sticking my tongue out back at her.

She chooses to ignore me, and continues to fall all over Tom, who seems happy with the attention he is getting.

Chris is now in the hole they have been digging, and Mira is happily burying her little brother. It's deep enough now that his body is buried up to the top of his belly button. Mira is currently pushing more sand over his waist and legs.

"Can I help?" I ask.

"Yeah!" they both exclaim.

I'm digging out the sand at Chris's back so it's more comfortable for him, when I get the strangest feeling that we are being watched. It grows more and more intense.

A large gust of wind blows past me, whipping my hair across my face. I try frantically to control it as I look around. That's when I see it, there in the bushes across from us.

An orange glow highlights three large, yellow eyes that stare at us. The creature notices I am aware of its presence, and slowly the creature creeps forward out of the bushes, and stalks towards us.

The beast is the size of a very large bear. It's body is a mixture of armored scales, jet black fur, and crystals that are pulsing a deep orange glow.

Each of its four, thick legs glow brightly, lined with three large, orange crystal spikes. I look around, no one else seems to notice it.

How can that be? It's HUGE! First this morning, now this! Am I going insane? My eyes are fixed on the beast stalking towards us.

"What's wrong, Aunty Bree?" Chris asks.

The creature's three eyes dart to Chris and Mira. Abruptly, I jump to my feet, grabbing Chris under his arms freeing him from the sand. Placing him down in one swift movement, I force them both behind me, with my arms outstretched, shielding them from its view, it raises its head glaring at me. Mira begins to panic.

"What's wrong, Aunty Bree? You're acting weird," she bleats out in a panic.

Chris moves his head around me, trying to see what I see, but confusion sets on his face when he sees......nothing?

With Mira and Chris behind me, and my arms outstretched to shield them, my eyes fixed on something.

Mia and Tom have stopped their fawning. They both look over toward us. Mia slides off Tom's lap and starts walking over to us cautiously.

"DO NOT MOVE!" I yell, not taking my eyes of the beast.

Mia stops dead in her tracks. Mira is frightened by my sudden outburst and runs for her mother.

"NO!" I scream.

The beast launches itself after her. I run to catch up, not thinking at all. The only thought that runs through my mind is cutting it off before it gets to her.

I throw myself behind Mira as the beast reaches her, connecting with it. Twisting my body, I throw my arms around its neck, slamming into it with a heavy thud, the impact throwing it off course away from Mira. The creature bucks and pulls at me trying to make me let go.

It swipes a massive paw at me, the claws connecting, ripping my shirt. Four long slice marks appear across my stomach, my crimson blood splashing across the creature's face.

Mia and Tom gasp, as they know something is not right. I'm not insane. Mia scoops Mira into her arms, and Tom has reached Chris.

Mia pauses, looking at me as I'm thrown to the ground. The creature shakes its head, relieved to be free of me. The beast prepares itself to come at me again.

"BREE!" Mia yells scared and bewildered.

"RUN, GETAWAY, DON'T WORRY ABOUT ME!" I yell.

Tom has bundled his family in his arms, trying to pull Mia and the kids towards the car. Mia's frozen, her eyes fixed on me, fear flooding her face. She won't move. I have to get it away from my sister and her family.

Heart racing, I quickly look around. If only I had something to defend myself with. The image of a long, thick, silver dagger I had seen in one of my dreams comes to mind. In an instance, a blue glow appears in my right hand and there it is, the dagger I was just thinking of.... 'What the?'

Pushing all my questions and thoughts aside, I run towards it, throwing my arm out, and thrusting the dagger into the creature's chest. It roars a loud howl of pain as the dagger breaches the tough armored skin.

The beast throws itself up onto its hind legs, thrashing to swipe the dagger free from its chest. I take this moment, while it is distracted, to propel forward, throwing myself into the creature's waist as hard as I can.

Standing on its hind legs, it's at least twice the height of me now. I wrap my arms around its torso as we connect, throwing it down with everything I have.

I hear the screams of my family behind me as I knock the creature off its feet. It's massive paws flail, trying to stop itself from succumbing to the force of my tackle. No one hurts my family! I need to get it away from them!

The moment the thought enters my mind, a blue glow surrounds me, bright, white, light floods my eyes, blinding me. I feel myself falling, the sounds of my family's cries are becoming further and further away, until I can't hear them anymore.

I'm still falling, and the feel of the creature still clawing and thrashing underneath me, making me aware it's still with me, unsure of what's going on. I tighten my grip around the creature's waist. It swipes frantically again. This time, it's claws
find me, connecting with my flesh. I feel them tear at my back.

"Ahh...." pain shoots through my body.

It swipes again, and again, clawing at my back and shoulders. I keep my head tucked in, holding on tight, trying to block out the pain with everything I have.

This thing is going to kill me if I don't stop it somehow. I remember the steel dagger that is still embedded in the creature's chest.

I push myself up towards the dagger, still holding tight to the beast, reaching up a little further, my hand trails up through its thick fur and scales, feeling my way until my fingers brush against the cool metal. With a firm grasp on the dagger, I pull myself up a little more, and using all my weight, I force it in further. I feel the resistance from the creature's tough skin slowly give way.

I can feel it puncturing through layer by layer of fat, tissue, and muscle. The creature flails harder, desperate to separate itself from my assault. The dagger sinks deeper and deeper, it's fighting begins to weaken.

My heartbeat is vibrating through my body, my breath stinging in my throat. I take a deep breath, and hold it through clenched teeth. I push harder at the dagger until I feel it cannot go any further.

The creature's flailing is like weak bats now. It's paws smack at my back one last time. This time its claws are withdrawn, too weak to hold their weight. Its paws slide off my back and drop to its side then…. nothing.

-

2

The Bond

The blinding light is fading now and my vision is clearing. I hope Mia and the others are okay. I blink a few times to correct my vision, looking around for my family.

Instead, I find myself in a large, old style banquet hall full of people, all sitting at long, calved, wooden tables, topped with illustrious mounds of food and drink, realizing I'm in the middle of one......straddling the beast.

Where am I? Who are these people? What is this creature? Where did it come from? Why did it attack me and my family? What was that light? How did that dagger appear, and where did it go once the creature had died? I have so many questions running around my head, with no sign of answers.

Three long, large, thickly carved wooden tables are perfectly parallel to each other. A long regal looking table at the top overlooks the whole room, I assume where the higher-ups sit.

Slowly I become more aware of my surroundings. The copper smell that breaches my nose makes me realize I'm covered in blood, the creature's...and I believe my own. I am in the center of a room, on a dining table, in the middle of what looks to be a celebration.... This can't look natural!

People begin to buzz around me, talking in a tongue I can't understand. From the higher-up's table, a large man in his late fifties rises from a large throne of red velvet, trimmed with thick gold.

He is reasonably good looking, tall with broad shoulders, and a small waist. His hair has soft swifts of grey that highlight his shoulder-length, dark brown hair, a short beard neatly lines his mouth and chin.

He is wearing tight-fitting black leather pants and a white shirt. His purple and silver silk waistcoat is fastened with four big, silver buttons up the front, that peeks through from under a long thick overcoat with a high collar, and perched neatly at his throat a deep purple top knot sits.

The gentleman has a soft look about him... *A familiar look*, I think to myself.

Striding towards me, his overcoat dances around his ankles. He walks with a very handsome man next to him... my eyes widen in surprise ....It's him! The man I saw in my dream.

This morning, when I saw this man, I was full of hate. I could feel it burning deep within me, an overwhelming desire to destroy him.

Nervously, I watch in silence, gauging him as he approaches me. His eyes don't leave mine as he makes his way down between the two long tables to where I am, still frozen, straddling the beast.

His eyes assess me with a hint of annoyance and slight intrigue. The man holds his head proudly, clasping his hands together at his back, alongside his king. He walks towards me, the king seems excited somehow, while the man doesn't seem impressed at all.

They both reach me at the same time, stopping just short of my position. The king says something directed at me, I assume. I stay quiet, staring wide-eyed, and confused as hell, as I have no idea what to say or do.

He lets out a light laugh, I believe at my expense. The man beside him whispers something quietly to him, and the king looks at me again in a quizzical way. Then he laughs, shaking his head, waving off whatever he said.

The king steps towards me, reaching out a hand, I assume offering to help me down from the table. I gingerly take his hand as he guides me away from the beast to the floor. He looks me up and down, looking very amused and still holding my left hand gently as his examination of me continues.

My jeans are torn, and I can feel there isn't much left of the back of my new shirt, I already know there are four gashes in the front. A sigh escapes my lips as I can only imagine how I must look.

His eyes scan my face and settle on my eyes. I only remember the presence of the younger man when he takes a step forward. Instinctively, I snap my hand back, retreat a step away from him, and immediately regret it.

He freezes, cocking an eyebrow at me. My reaction has not pleased him in the slightest. He stays on his spot, not risking me running, I think. I'm grateful for this. He folds his arms across his chest as he continues to discuss me with the king.

My more than an obvious desire not to be near this man, I believe has caused concern. They continue talking about me. This continues for a while.

I hate not knowing what's going on. The king seems to be agitated, and I believe, so is his younger companion. As he rests his right hand on his hip, he throws his left hand agitatedly into his hair.... He's annoyed.

My stance becomes rigid. He shoots a glare at me. Shooting forward, he grabs me around my waist with his right hand, stopping me from retreating again. He grabs my chin with his left hand quickly, and quite rough. I'm shocked by the sudden contact.

He has me. *What do I do? I have nowhere to run. Is he going to hurt me?* Everywhere he's touching feels like it's on fire, and the closeness of his face to mine is making me very aware of him. He's staring into my eyes. They seem to intrigue him, as they did the king. I feel his breath clashing with mine. He's so close!

My body starts shaking. In that instant, a shock shoots through my body. My blue light is around me again, but brighter this time. It feels different from before, this time, it feels like my magic is reaching out to him. He's surrounded by purple light, it's beautiful.

Our colors reach out for one another, our eyes transfixed, both of us frozen, unable to move. My heart is beating out of my chest. I can feel his, too, it's beating just as hard as mine. My head begins to spin with, pictures, places, memories...

I can't break away from the hold we are in. Still locked in place, unable to break away, blue and purple twist around us in a seductive dance of bright color, like they were two lovers who had finally found each other after so long, twisting like a rope around each other molding into one, wrapping us, tighter, closer, until our bodies are pressed together with no space left between us.

Our lights begin to fade, until finally, we find ourselves able to move again. A look of horror has appeared on his face. He quickly drops his hand from my chin, and takes a big step back from me. Running his hands down his face, then pushing them into his hair, where they rest on his head. The whole room was silently staring at us.

The room starts to spin, slowly getting faster. I don't know if my injuries have finally caught up with me, or if it's everything that has happened so far. I feel the room go dark. I begin to fall. The last thing I hear is...

"A BOND HAS BEEN MADE!"

3

Light magic

"HOW CAN THIS BE? I WON'T ACCEPT THIS!" A man's voice says.

"You can't change a bond my son," another man's voice retorts.

"THE HELL I CAN'T!" he bites back.

"A bond is absolute, it can't be ignored and it can't be broken. Most people go through life never finding their bond, think yourself lucky," he argues.

"LUCKY! You saw her color! She is Verillian, how can I be bound to that? Not to mention light magic has never been bonded outside of light magic before. It's not supposed to work this way, I refuse to believe this!" the man spits.

"The bond works in mysterious ways, my son, but it's never wrong," a voice says harshly.

Bond? Verillian? What are they talking about? Why can I understand them now? None of this makes any sense! My eyes flit open and I see them at the end of the bed, arguing with one another.

I'm in a rather large, wooden, four poster bed. I go to sit up, but realize I'm not wearing any clothes, and quickly sink back down under the covers, in a heavy mix of assorted furs, and thick woolen blankets. He turns, realizing I'm awake. The king smiles at me fondly and inclines his head slightly in my direction.

"You must have a lot of questions my dear. I'll leave you with my son to discuss in private, we can chat later at dinner," the king says softly, still smiling. He turns and leaves the room.

We are alone now. Absentmindedly, he runs a hand through his shaggy, black hair. He looks tired, perplexed, and most of all, defeated. He undoes the buckle of the waist strap that holds his sword and sheath at his left hip, and places it on the chair next to the door. He sits on the end of the bed, his forearms resting on his legs as he drops his gaze to the floor. Silence falls, but is soon broken.

"I don't like this any more than you do. I'm gathering, but what can we do?" he says in a quiet, defeated tone, still looking at the floor.

"I....I have no idea what you're talking about," I say in a quiet, cracked tone. "Where am I?"

"This is the Nigalia kingdom of creature magic," he replies.

"Who are you?" I ask.

He raises an eyebrow to me. "Prince Aiden, son of King Darnell and Queen Reina. And You are from Verillia Kingdom," he says.

"Umm, what? *No,* I'm from San Diego, "I say, bewildered.

He looks at me, confused. "I have never heard of this San Diego. Do they have light magic, too?" he asks.

"I'm sorry, I don't know what light magic is, or even creature magic, either. Nothing you have said makes any sense to me, and another thing, how come I can understand you all of a sudden?" I say, a little too quickly, and a little breathless.

"I believe that would be because of the bond," Aiden replies.

"The what?" I ask.

"The bond," he repeats. He looks at me for a moment, as if saying, *'do I really have to explain this?'*

I keep a stern look on my face as I continue to look back at him. He shakes his head, and runs his hands through his hair. I assume he does this a lot when he's frustrated. Defeated, he lets out a sigh.

"The bond is a rare occurrence. It's where two bodies of magic connect with one another," he says quickly.

Aiden looks at me with an expression of hope that his explanation has satisfied my question. From the look on my face, he knows I'm more lost than ever.

"Have you ever heard of the story about how all humans were born with two heads, four arms, and four legs, a god became fearful of their power, so he filled the sky with lightning bolts, raining them down onto the planet, separating all the humans, right down the middle so that they would roam the world for the rest of eternity searching for their other half?" he asks.

"Yes, I have heard something like that," I say, somewhat intrigued.

"The bond is like that. It is said to be the bonding of two bodies of magic. Only those who possess magic can make a magical bond. If the bond is ignored and paired with another not intended, the magic line dies, but when they find each other, and embrace the bond, the magic line continues, far more powerful than before."

"As you can imagine, it doesn't happen a lot. The only magic lines that are left are; creature magic, the ability to tame and control creatures, big and small. Creature magic is not all about magic though, there is far less magic involved with creature magic. Then there is elemental magic, which is the ability to control one of the four elements. Fire, Earth, and Wind. Water is spoken of but has not been seen in hundreds of years. And the very endangered light magic... Which you possess. Light magic is feared above all else, because no one knows their magic's limitations," he explains. "The only ones to possess magic are of royal blood. When magic was first born, those with magic were considered royalty, and most magic that was born was inside those magic lines. Occasionally, magic has been found outside of a royal family line, and they are instantly integrated into the royal household, but we don't know enough about light magic to know if it is the same for your people. How did you get here?" Aiden asks.

"I can't say how or where I'm from originally, as I was found at the age of twelve, by a boathouse in San Diego, with no memory of my past, a place far more different from here," I answer.

He looks at me for a moment, then says, "The soul princess of Verillia, went missing at the age of twelve, right before a large-scale attack was made on their kingdom. Long brown hair, and lavender eyes, like no other. Coincidence? I don't think so...lavender eyes have only ever been seen once and you have lavender eyes," Aiden says.

"Are you trying to tell me I'm some lost princess with endangered magic no one knows about and I'm originally from this land?" I say with amusement.

He gives me a stern look, stopping me from continuing my rant.

I think over all that he has told me. Honestly, the more I think about it the more it seems possible, and somehow, I know he's telling me the truth, I can feel it.

"This explains a few things, but opens a lot more questions. How you ended up in the other place and managed to just appear before a room full of people, in the middle of our feast, atop of a dead Akuma, is the question I want to know most of all. If your magic was capable of this then why here? Why now?" he says in a ramble.

"I just want to go back home tell me how and ill leave and you won't have to worry about me anymore" I say hopefully.

Aiden laughs "Haven't you been listening? there is no magic we know of that could have brought you here, your magic brought you here, so obviously your magic is what will send you back" I move to sit myself up again, and a flood of new questions come back to mind.

"Where are my clothes? And why am I undressed?" I ask.

Realization hits him hard as he jumps off the bed and turns his back to me. Aiden clears his throat...

"Oh... um, when you passed out from the loss of blood, I caught you and brought you here. You needed to be cleaned up so our healer could see to your wounds. Before you can heal Akuma wounds they must be cleansed, as their blood turns to acid if not treated in time," he says in a rush. "There was no salvaging your clothes at all, I'm afraid, but there is suitable attire for you in the cupboard over there," he says quickly, waving to a tall grand cupboard on the other side of the room. "I'll wait out in the hall and leave you to get dressed," he says a little embarrassed. He turns to leave, but stops abruptly at the door with his back to me.

"When you first saw me, you acted as if you recognized me...but you seemed afraid.... Why?" he quietly asks.

"Uh... I don't know...." I lie.

Aiden is not happy with my reply, but seems to accept my answer. He opens the door and leaves me to dress. Once the door is closed, I get up, wrapping one of the fur blankets around me, and walk to the cupboard.

It's tall, and beautifully carved with vines, trees, and butterflies. I see a squirrel, owl, and some other birds. It's beautiful, I feel if I open this door, I might find a mystic land on the other side, I chuckle at the thought as I realize I am already in one.

I run my fingers over a butterfly. I think of my sister and what she must be going through right now. I just disappeared. The thought is uninviting, and it hurts my chest. I snap my thoughts back and open the cupboard door.

There are at least a dozen beautifully made dresses, made of the finest silks, satins, furs, and velvets, trimmed with fine lace and beautiful ribbons. I choose a lovely blue dress that skims the floor. It's trimmed with silver lace and white pearls. The overcoat is open at the top and has three big buttons under the breast line, leaving the topcoat open at the bottom as well. I adjust the high collar and smooth out the dress, satisfied.

I make my way to the door. When I open it, Aiden is there waiting for me. When he sees me, his eyes dart over my attire, analyzing my choice. I give Aiden a little twirl, showcasing the dress.

"I guess that will do. Follow me to the dining hall," he says, seemingly satisfied with my attire, I assume.

I feel more comfortable around him than I did before, which I find strange, but there is still that image that I can't shake and it makes me uneasy.

I'm walking behind him taking in my surroundings. The ceilings are high, and the dark halls are lit with floating orbs of glowing light.

When we reach a huge door at the end, he stops and I almost run into the back of him. He waves his hand and it opens immediately, with a slow long creek that reverberates through the hall.

We step into the room. It's nowhere near as big as the banquet hall, but it's still impressive. The orbs line the high ceilings, and a group of them are bundled in the center of the large carved wooden table, a lot like the ones in the banquet hall, only carved better with exquisite craftsmanship. The walls are draped with tapestries, and banners here and there.

Aiden directs me to a seat next to the king. I sit quietly as he pushes my chair in.

"Thank you," I say quietly.

He seems taken back by my words, but shakes it off almost immediately. Without a word, he nods at me, and leaves to take his seat.

When King Darnell arrives, Aiden is seated across from me and his father sits at the very top between us both. The appearance of his father has not brought him back from wherever he is, seeming lost in thought.

"Aiden," his father calls as he reaches to rest a hand on his shoulder.

"My apologies, father," Aiden says, bringing his attention back to greet him.

"Quite alright, my son. We have all been through a lot today. Now, how are you feeling my dear?" he asks in my direction.

"Much better thank you. I still have many questions," I say politely.

"I'm sure you do, as do we," replies the king.

"Could you first explain how you managed to appear in our hall with a dead Akuma?" he asks.

I take a deep breath and explain my run-in with the creature at the park, and all that happened until the moment I found myself in their hall. They both look from one to the other. The king is the first to break the silence.

"To be honest, it's impressive that anyone could survive an Akuma attack and live to tell the tale. You must really be something," he says, amused and a little impressed.

"Akuma are very dark, very powerful, and they are only found in the Capium fields in the north. Capium is a very powerful and dangerous material used in dark magic. Being exposed to it causes them to glow orange and it gives them incredible size and strength," he says.

"I don't know how such a dangerous creature was able to cross realms, especially since it is rare for anyone to do, but not impossible.

I believe light magic sent it to you and your magic brought it back, sending you with it. Light magic has been seen to materialize things with a simple thought, so your dagger you spoke of makes sense. It disappeared when it's use was fulfilled. We can't explain much about your magic, as very little is known, I'm afraid," he adds.

"My having light magic, as you say, seems to upset everyone. Why?" I ask.

Aiden shifts uncomfortably in his chair. He goes to say something but stays quiet as his father glowers at him.

"Varillia has been at war with all magic for a long time, as they believed light magic should be the only magic, seeing all others as inferior. This angered the other kingdoms. As a result, they all banded together to wipe Varillia out. It was believed they had succeeded, until I noticed your lavender eyes. I thought you may be the missing princess and when your magic was revealed. When the bond was made, I was even more certain," the king says joyfully. "Speaking of which, we will have to hold the ceremony soon."

"What ceremony?" I ask.

"The one where we join you in front of the people. The news of your bond has exploded around the kingdom, it's all anyone is talking about, especially when light magic was thought to be extinct and has never been known to bond with any magic, other than its own before," he says excitedly waving his hands around the room.

"When you say ceremony..." I pause for a moment. "You mean like a marriage?"

"Well, a bond is far greater than any marriage, but... yes," he smiles at me. A cold chill runs through my body.

"I can't marry him! I don't know him!" I shout.

"You're already married, and it was witnessed in a room full of people at the banquet hall. This is only a ceremony for the people. If you were already married, the bond would supersede it and the marriage would be null and void," he states.

I'm stunned into silence. I cannot put my thoughts or words together. This morning I was single, powerless, and moping around my apartment in San Diego with my family nearby, oblivious to anything else.

Now, I'm married, or should I say, bonded, to a man who hates me, in a land I don't know, surrounded by people who hate me, magic and customs I don't understand, and strange creatures that want me dead and no way home. This may take a while to process. I look over at Aiden who is looking down at his hands.

"How can you be so calm about all this?" I say a little too harshly.

He sharply slams both his hands down on the table, making me jump. "What choice do I have? I have about as much say in this as you do!" he snarls at me through gritted teeth. He recovers himself and relaxes a little after a sharp look from his father. "Going against this is a death sentence to our magic line and the very core of our being. I have come to accept it and so should you," He says in a bitter undertone.

"But you don't even like me, I heard you say so! There is so much I need to know before I can even start accepting this," I say sharply.

"Like it or not, we have no choice."

I scowl at him but say nothing, we finish the rest of dinner in silence.

"I'm off to bed now. It's been a long day. I suggest you two do the same," the king says. Aiden rises from his seat.

"Training will start tomorrow, bright and early, we better get some rest," Aiden agrees.

"What training?" I ask.

"You are now my bonded wife," he hisses.

I flinch at the word wife.

"In this family, every one of us protects our people with the gifts we are blessed with, and no wife of mine will be an embarrassment to our family name," he glares at me. "This is not negotiable" he warns folding his arms across his chest.

I'm annoyed. Really annoyed. I frown at him. I want to explode at him, but I keep my mouth shut.

We walk back to our room in silence. We are both uncomfortable with this, and certainly not happy. We reach the room we will now share as husband and wife for the foreseeable future, or until I can find a way back home.

Aiden opens the door and lets me pass. I walk over to the side of the bed that has a set of draws with an assortment of undergarments and nightwear for me.

Wow they're quick, I think to myself. I gingerly open the draw looking for a nightgown and find some in the second draw.

I pull the white lace nightgown from the draw and see Aiden

undressing cautiously, eyeing me as he undoes his buttons until his torso is bare before me. He slides his shirt off his shoulders and drapes it over the chair by the door.

Wow, he's magnificent, I gape, trying hard not to show I'm looking. He sits on the end of the bed with his toned back to me, to wrestle with his boots and socks.

I take this chance to start undressing into my nightgown. I manage to get the overcoat off, and as I bring my dress over my head, I noticed Aiden glance at me over his shoulder. I stop and hold the fabric close to my chest. He quickly turns his head and stands to unbuckle his belt.

I quickly drop the dress, throwing the lace nightgown over my head in one swift movement, then dive under the safety of the covers. He looks over at me as he starts to unbutton his pants, I turn over in the bed, looking away and sinking my face into the pillow.

I hear a clank of metal and pat of cloth hit the cobblestone floor, the sound of him placing his boots between the legs of the chair, and draping his pants with his shirt and coat.

I feel the bed lower as his weight sinks onto the bed beside me. I hope he's not expecting anything from me, the thought makes me nervous.

I feel him shift and I pull the cover tighter around me. He's lying beside me, looking up at the ceiling when I feel his gaze pricking at the back of my neck. I pull the covers up under my nose.

A sudden movement shocks me, as he gets up abruptly and grabs a bunch of pillows from the floor, stuffing them between us and climbs back in beside me. A little relieved, I lower the covers and settle in. It's been a long, emotional day and it's not long before I find the sweet release of sleep.

4

Training

A shiver runs through me. I slide my leg up the bed searching for warmth. I feel movement brush past my skin, sliding up between my legs. A strong arm crosses my waist, pulling me close, into the warmth I was searching for. Content, I fall back to sleep.

The light flows into the room and my warmth begins to stir around me. Slowly, I open my eyes and find myself nestled into Aiden's chest, his arms wrapped around my shoulders and waist, our legs wrapped together, with his chin resting on the top of my head.

Realization hits, and I'm afraid to move and wake him. How do I get out of this? I move my legs slightly and find some of the pillows that at one point separated us. The others must have been tossed out in our search for warmth through the night.

Slowly I try moving his hand from my waist. He stirs, pulling me tighter into him. He mumbles something incoherently, nuzzling his face into my hair. He continues to sleep. I move to try again, when a knock at the door startles us both.

"Prince Aiden? It's six am, breakfast will be served in half an hour," a voice calls through the door.

"I'm awake, be there shortly," Aiden calls out half asleep. The hand around my waist releases me to rub his face.

He slowly opens his eyes, looking down at me for a moment. I look back at him. His eyes trail down the bed and up again.

He quickly releases his arm that still holds me to him, retreating slowly from the center of the bed, where I assume, we have been in each other's arms for most of the night. A little disoriented, he lifts the covers and swings his legs out of the bed.

"Get dressed for breakfast and make sure you wear something you can easily move around in," he says groggily, breaking the silence. Aiden dresses quickly, leaving me alone to dress, which I find myself grateful for.

Breakfast is quiet, and a bit awkward. It looks like Aiden and I are the only ones here. I don't see anyone except the young ladies that serve us. They work quickly, not meeting my gaze but I notice them steal glances at Aiden.

"Does the king have his breakfast later?" I ask the server reaching for my empty plate and cup. She gasps, and knocks them to the ground, shattering the plate and chipping the cup when I address her.

Panicked, she looks at the floor, then at me as she backs away, then turns and retreats back to the kitchen without answering my question. I look down at the broken pieces, realizing how hard things are going to be for me here.

After a few moments, Aiden gets up and beckons me to follow

him. We walk through the long halls in silence. At the end, two large, wooden doors with iron handles open as we approach. The light floods the dark entrance, and we step out into the courtyard.

Aiden walks ahead of me to an open space of sand, circled by a wooden fence. All along the fence line are different weapons of all types, shapes, and sizes. From wooden swords, and staffs, to iron shields, spears, maces, and a few I don't recognize.

Aiden walks over, and takes off his coat and shirt. He drapes them over the fence, then walks the perimeter of the mini-battle field to a large selection of quarterstaffs. Testing a few, he seems to settle on two, abruptly tossing one to me. I scramble to catch it in time, marginally avoiding being hit in the face. He walks toward me with a long, heavy looking staff in hand.

"Is it comfortable?" he asks, in an absent tone, referring to the weapon in my hands no doubt.

I run my hands up its smooth finish, and tighten my grip as I feel its weight.

"It's light. I guess so," I reply.

"Good, let's begin." Aiden says lowering his staff to the ground, then comes at me full force, sweeping his staff at my feet taking me down hard!

"Oof! Oh my god. Is that how you teach someone? You attack them straight up?" I grumble slowly lifting my head.

He walks over and crouches down beside me with a cocky look on his face. "Hm, interesting." he says with analytic amusement.

"What's so damn interesting?" I retort, my annoyance evident.

"Well, I figured a bond would share our abilities somehow, but it doesn't seem as though you got this one. I just find it interesting. Oh well, I guess the long way it is. Dust yourself off and get up. looks like this will take longer than I had hoped, but then again, I didn't have high expectations in the first place," he taunts.

Boiling with rage, and the desire to put this big-mouthed ass on his snide backside, I hastily get back up on my feet. I do pole dancing, and kickboxing every week, it shouldn't be too hard to use all I have learned and combine it with a staff.

We sidestep the pit area, not taking our eyes off each other. I know he's not going to take it easy on me, and in some way, I feel like he's enjoying this a little more than he's letting on. He has an opportunity to smack me around for a bit. Yeah, he's enjoying this alright, and I'm in no way inclined to let him have his way if I can help it.

Aiden is the first to move as he leaps forward at me. Damn he's fast. I barely see him move, but just as he goes to sweep me again, I manage to jump, quickly sidestepping away from him. Okay, I managed to dodge that one.

Thank you, Tom, I think to myself, remembering our brutal training sessions together. He never went easy on me either. Mia never approved of me going any place alone and always worried for my safety. After Tom started training with me, she seemed much more easy going. All I have to do is just keep my wits about me. I'm brought back from my thoughts when Aiden looks at me with a wicked smile spreading across his face.

"This should be interesting," he says.

"Oh crap."

Again, he launches at me, faster than before, and no surprise, I end up on my ass again. Over and over the brutal assault continues, as I improve with each match.

Aiden gets faster every time. I focus everything I have just to match his pace. He swings a blow to my side and I manage to block it, but counters with a whack to my butt. I look at his wide grin as I rub my backside.

"There's more where that came from," he says, cockily twirling his staff.

I shoot him a scowl.

"We are the only kingdom that focuses on our bodies and our magic. We can't expect to train creatures if we aren't prepared to do the same, and as we don't wield elements. Our training alleviates the slight disadvantage we have," he adds.

"If I'm so powerful I shouldn't need this then," I smirk.

"With your knowledge at the moment, I wouldn't turn down any improvements," he retorts dryly, taking my feet from under me again.

Again, and again, our two staffs collide. I manage to block him each time, as he comes at me harder and harder, my breath burning in my throat.

I am unsure of how I'm blocking his strikes, I'm just grateful I am. He comes at me again, and again. Getting faster each time. He changes direction, sweeping upward, ejecting my staff from my hands.

I miss him going for a leg sweep, resulting in my legs swiftly coming out from underneath me. The force rocks through me as I hit the sand with a violent thud winding me.

I see his staff come down. Squeezing my eyes shut, I gasp for breath, waiting for the final blow. I wait for a few beats of my racing heart, my breath coming back to me. Slowly, I open my eyes. His staff has stopped, just above my nose.

"Again," he commands, stepping back, returning to his battle stance.

Over the next few days, this becomes our normal routine. The only thing now is, my goal isn't to beat him. I just focus on staying on my feet, until the inevitable moment he puts me on my ass again.

"Ooof," I hit the ground again, surely adding a few new bruises to my rapidly growing collection.

"Shock horror on your back again? Honestly, I don't know why I even bother with you," Aiden says dryly.

I get back up slowly, feeling every bit worse for wear. As I do so, he is attacking me again the moment I am on my feet, blow after blow, until I feel the structure of the weapon give way. CRACK! The pieces fly from my hands.

Aiden pushes through, knocking me to the ground, but this time he still comes at me. Panic rushes through me, the desire for my weapon to be between us desperately floods my thoughts.

A burst of blue light briefly blinds me. I blink a few times to find Aiden's face a breath from my own, a look of shock gracing his gorgeous features. It takes me a moment to realize I'm holding him back with a glowing staff of blue light. I know I need to get him off me. I take in a deep breath and throw my right knee up as hard as I can, sharply connecting it into his ribs, forcing him off me, giving me the time to get back on my feet.

"Well, maybe this bond thing isn't such a pile of rubbish," he grunts, rubbing his ribs.

I run towards him, but as I get close, Aiden changes his stance, readying himself to attack me. In one swift movement, I dig the staff into the sand, vaulting myself out of his reach.

I keep my grip firm, and swing my weight back around, planting my feet in between his shoulder blades, knocking him face down into the sand.

"Bond with that," I say, dropping my staff next to him.

As it hits the floor its form scatters and disappears. I walk away feeling pretty damn proud of myself. I've had enough training for one day. I'll deal with the fallout later. I hear Aiden chuckle, as he flips over still laying in the sand. I don't look back, I just walk away.

The stone path stretches on, but my feet seem to know where they're going. Large trees with leaves of red and gold line the way. I follow it until I come to a large opening. My breath catches as a magnificent bloom tree fills my view. I know this place.

5

The Bloom Tree

It's been a few days now, and every day starts the same, me in Aiden's arms, the fortress we build up each night destroyed by morning, Aiden's torture sessions, and then he disappears, and everyone avoids me.

"Ah, Bree, just the lovely, young lady I was looking for," the king calls out grabbing my attention.

"Oh, Your Majesty, I'm sorry. I didn't see you there," I reply.

"Oh, that's quite alright, my dear. I'm just glad I caught you, it's hard to find you these days," he says with a smile.

"Oh? I didn't know you were looking for me. I like to go for a little wonder after my torture session with Aiden each morning," I say with a light chuckle.

"Ah yes, I have heard you have gotten quite good and can stand well against him, sometimes even getting the better of him, too," he grins widely at me.

I blush slightly, knowing full well he's talking about the few times I have managed to catch him off guard with a few moves, but he adjusts quickly, never falling for the same trick twice. Sometimes he uses my moves back on me. I grimace at the thought.

"Will you allow me to escort you a little of the way? I won't trouble you for long, my dear," he asks sweetly.

"Yes, of course, you could never trouble me, Your Majesty. You seem to be the only friendly face I have around here at the moment, so I find you a breath of fresh air," I answer back.

"Oh, it thrills me you feel that way," he chuckles. "The main reason I have come to find you, is to give you this," he says, handing me a large, old book. "This came into my possession when I went to see my brother in the east, and I thought it might help you with learning about your magic. There is no one here who can help you learn about your magic and how to control it. There is nothing dangerous in it so I didn't see any harm in you having it," he adds.

"I haven't even tried to use my magic, as I find it upsets people," I say, a little disheartened.

"Oh, my dear it's just fears of the unknown, and I know you will make them see how beautiful light magic can be. I don't believe anything bad could ever come from such a treasure," he reassures me.

I blush and can't help but smile. "Okay, I'll read it and try my best to prove you right," I say with more confidence than I have felt in a while.

"Ah, now that's what I was hoping for." He presses a kiss to my forehead. "Okay, I'll leave you be now, but can I ask one little favor of you?" he asks.

"Of course, anything," I smile.

"Could you keep this just between us?" he motions to the book in my hand. "I only ask this of you, because this book was supposed to be destroyed after the kingdom fell, but I could not bring myself to see it done," he confesses.

"Oh, yes, of course. This will be our little secret," I smile, clutching the book to my chest.

He returns my smile, nods, and leaves.

I reach the bloom tree and sit beneath its immense shade. The book King Darnell gave me is a little bigger than an A4 piece of paper and thicker than an entire works of Shakespeare.

The cover is leather bound with silver embossed words that say 'M and L Introduction to Light Magic.' In the center is a blue jewel. The pages are old and a little faded, but for its age it's very well preserved.

I turn to the first page, and I see in bold letters, *How to Summon a Deerling.*

Deerlings are light companions that teach its conjurer concentration. They are used for training focus for multiple castings, and longer holds. To summon, simply follow these steps.

I look through the first few pages and notice a picture of what looks a bit like a deer, but unbelievably cute, with big, baby eyes and five long smoke-like tails. I return to the instructions, rotating my hands as it tells me to. After I have the motions down, I return my attention to the picture.

I try over and over, but nothing happens. Determined, I start to look at the deerlings five tails. They look like they would gracefully glide behind it as it moves.

I imagine its movements as if it were real and not just a picture. I raise my hands and do the movements again, rotating my right hand over my left ever so slightly. A light glow of blue appears in front of me, and out of it steps a small deerling that could fit in the palm of my hand.

Day after day, I return to the tree with my book, always starting with conjuring my deerling. Slowly, I learn how to keep my focus while doing other things as well. It doesn't take long before it becomes second nature to me and my deerling begins to do things on its own. After a while, it would play in my hair or perch itself on my shoulder as I read my book, even curl up on my knee and rest for a while.

The rest of the book is filled with a huge array of things, like conjuring creatures of different uses, weapons, and other objects, creating illusions, barriers, and recipes for curing ailments and injuries. I even found one to increase your power for a short time. I know the book has a few secrets, since I find new things appear in it all the time, and every now and then when I flip through the blank pages at the back, I swear I have seen words appear, but they always vanish when I flip back. I would not have thought much of it if it didn't keep happening.

I look down at my lap and find my deerling curled up on my knee asleep. I smile and stroke it gently with my fingers, his ears twitch slightly but he continues to sleep peacefully.

I'm running as fast as I can down the cobblestone path, his hot on my tail but he won't beat me this time. I push myself forward, driven by determination. The trees flash past me in a blur of red and gold. I cut across the hedges at the T-junction towards my destination.

Yes, there it is! I'll beat him this time!

As the bloom tree comes into view, a small boy of about ten flies out from the trees on my left. Damn it, how can he be so fast? Moments before I reach the tree, he touches it first.

"Yes! I beat you again, Bree! Ha-ha!" he shouts.

"That's no fair, your legs are longer than mine!" I shout back.

"Oh, those are just excuses," he retorts breathlessly. Bellamina his Bupper pup has caught up to him and is now enjoying a belly rub while she recovers from her run with us.

"Okay, okay. You win again. I so thought I had you this time," I whine, flopping on my back catching my breath.

"How long do we have to play today?" the boy asks, catching his breath, too.

"Father is away on business for a couple of days, and Alice will be far too busy cleaning up a little mishap in the basement, and won't be looking for me until at least noon, so I have until then," I announce proudly.

"All right!" the boy exclaims, seeming revitalized by my news. "What do you want to do today? We have to make the most of it," he says, clapping his hands together.

I laugh. "Oh, I know! I know! I want to play with the butterflies again!" I exclaim excitedly.

"Oh, not that again," he rolls his eyes at me.

"Awe, come on! I love watching you with the animals. *Please,*" I beg, with the biggest eyes my face will allow.

He thinks for a moment. "Hm, what about something new?"

"Yes, yes, yes!" I say, clapping my hands together in excitement as I bounce on my knees.

His face quickly changes to pure concentration.

I giggle.
"Shh!" he says, irritated. "I can't concentrate if you're making noises," the boy scolds.

I place my hands over my mouth to keep from giggling again.

He rolls his hands over and over, changing direction here and there. When a purple mist begins to reach out from his hands towards the trees, I lean forward waiting to see what will happen next.

I look around eagerly as two beautiful birds glide out from the trees flying straight through the mist. They glide effortlessly through the sky, barrel rolling and diving in a spectacular display as they fly around us.

One branches off, darting back through the trees and disappearing, while the other one flies closer and closer to me. Every time it circles back around, I am amazed and awestruck by its breathtaking beauty. Its large wings are a dazzling milk opal color.

I can't help but giggle in delight. My gaze follows the bird as it dances around me. My eyes land on the boy, whose smile is so bright and bursting with pride from his ability to entertain me. He holds out his arm, and the bird gracefully lands, allowing him to stroke its chest. I step towards him but stop abruptly when something flashes past me.

The other bird is back. It circles round and stops right in front of me. Gently, it beats its large, beautiful wings. In its beak, it holds a beautiful flower with velvet petals of stardust. Slowly, I reach forward and take it.

The moment I have the flower in my hand, they both fly off back into the trees. I look at the boy with a smile so wide it hurts. My chest restricts, and tears begin to roll down my face.

"Bree, Bree!" I wake up to Aiden's face hovering over me.

I look around and we are under the bloom tree. "I'm sorry, I must have fallen asleep," I say a little groggy.

"What are you doing here?" he asks.

"I've been coming here after training every day since I came across it," I resound.

"That certainly explains where you have been of late, but what made you come here?" he curiously asks.

"I don't know, I feel like I've been here before." I think for a moment about my dream, I wonder if that was a memory? I regain my thoughts. "Why do you ask?" I reply.

"No reason really, I was just curious. This is a beautiful place, it holds great memories for me," Aiden says gazing up at the tree, a calmness washing over him.

This is a gentle side I haven't seen before. It warms my heart, making me smile.

Collecting himself he looks down at me. "We better be getting back it's almost time for dinner."

Aiden helps me to my feet. I collect my things and we walk back down the path as if we had done it a thousand times before.

-

6

The Song

The following morning, Aiden is already gone. It's sometime after breakfast, judging from the sun. He didn't wake me. I find it strange since he seems to enjoy his usual morning torture sessions with me.

I get dressed, pulling on my brown leather pants, black boots, and white shirt. After I pack my book into my leather satchel, I decide to go to the kitchen to grab some food and drink for my visit to the bloom tree.

When I get to the kitchen it's quiet, too quiet. I move around the massive space. No one's here, how strange. I move around a corner and collide into a woman, knocking her and the culinary items she was carrying.

"I'm so sorry," I squeak, moving to help her up.

She stills when she sees me, a small yelp escaping her lips. I hold my hand out to her, encouraging her to take it, but she is looking at my hand as if it's going to grow legs and bite her.

I sigh. "Please, I didn't mean to knock you down. I understand you are wary of me, but please, let me help," I say quietly.

Cautiously, the woman takes my hand as I help her off the floor. Once up, she brushes her dress off and fixes her lovely, sun kissed locks, pinning a few loose strands back in her platted high bun. As she stands, her emerald eyes fix on me.

"Thank you," she says timidly. "I'm Madeline, is there something that brought you here?" she asks.

"Oh, yes. I only came to get myself some food. I slept in this morning and missed breakfast," I say, smiling at her.

"Of course, I'll grab you something right away," she replies.

"Oh, no. There is no need for you to create more work for yourself. I can manage." I say.

She seems shocked by my words and lowers her gaze from mine, stunned as to what to do or say.

"I'm sorry, I don't want to make more work for you. I just noticed your usual staff is not around." I wave my hand around at the empty kitchen.

"The rest of the staff are with His Majesty and the prince for the preparations for the ball tomorrow night. I get left behind all the time to struggle through on my own, so they can punish me when they return," she sighs.

"I have been around the castle very little, so it's no wonder I haven't noticed the preparations being made."

I look around and see all the work that Madeline is expected to do on her own when the kitchen usually has fifteen staff just for morning preparations. I smile when I get a brilliant idea. Before I begin, I decide to do something simple to gauge her reaction. I hold my hands out calling forth my deerling. In a little puff it prances out, cantering through the air over to Madeline.

She inhales deeply and goes rigid as it moves closer, stopping right in front of her. She watches as my deerling plays in front of her, as if begging her to play. Slowly Madeline softens, reaching out her hand she gingerly runs a shaking finger down its back. It nestles into her touch and she relaxes as a smile slowly spreads across her face.

With Madeline distracted, comfortably playing with my deerling, I decide to get to my task in mind. I think of the staff who usually help in the kitchen. The chef at the stove, Angela peeling the vegetables, Linda sweeping the floors, Monica baking the bread and Noreen preparing the meats, vividly bringing them all to life in my mind.

I raise my hands, casting forth my first multiple summons of fourteen helping hands for Madeline. Slowly, I open my eyes. Beautiful strings of shimmering blue, twist and curl, stretching out through the kitchen, forming into solid light copies of her kitchen companions. I hear Madeline inhale sharply at the sight of the copies working the kitchen, cleaning the mess from breakfast and doing the preparations for the afternoon. I stiffen, thinking of her reaction but keeping my concentration. Madeline slowly walks over to me, gaping at the sudden activity in the kitchen.

My deerling is happily on its back playing with Madeline's absent-minded fingers tickling its tummy.

"Are you okay?" I ask.

Madeline reaches my side, not taking her eyes off the copies busying themselves. She looks around, watching their shimmering forms work the daily tasks.

"I never knew you could do such things. This is amazing."

I relax, letting out the breath I didn't realize I had been holding.

Madeline joins the copies and directs me on what to make them do. I happily comply.

After an hour or so, most of the work is done and I find myself struggling to hold the forms much longer. Madeline notices and quickly comes to my side.

"My lady, it looks like this may have become too much for you. Most of the work is done, thanks to you and I'll have more than enough time to finish the rest on my own." She gently rests a hand on my shoulder with a soft smile.

I smile back at her and clear the copies. The moment the last one vanishes, I feel a huge weight lift from me, making me quite dizzy. I lose my footing for a moment and Madeline reaches out to steady me with a concerned expression on her face.

"I think you might have overdone it,"

"I'm sorry to worry you. It is my first time with so many. I haven't done more than three at a time before, but it's great to know I can do it. It just means I need more practice," I say, giving her a warm smile.

"I don't wish to give you orders, my lady, but I do think it might be best if you rest for a while," she says warmly.

"I do believe I will, but please, call me Bree. Thank you for the company and letting me practice in your kitchen. It has meant the world to me," I reply.

"Your company has been ... educational, but I do hope you won't make it a habit of doing my work for me, as you will put me out of a job," she chuckles.

"It's refreshing that you are worried about me and I thank you for that. As for my being here, we will keep it as our little secret, but you must promise to tell me the look on every one's faces when they see you have single handedly finished all the work," I chuckle.

"I promise," she replies with a full-body laugh.

I'm heading back to my room when I hear laughing. Curious, I turn the corner and follow the joyful sound. I stop at a large window that looks out over the manicured gardens and see Aiden playing with a group of children.

His soft smile and light-hearted laughs echo through the space, enchanting me completely. I stand and watch as the children run around him chasing the small chittle's he has trained for the kids to play with.

Their long fur covers their whole body, except their chubby round bellies that remain bare. Their big eyes and large pointy ears give them a cuteness that makes them easy to fall in love with.

An assortment of chittle colors flood the area, jumping in and out of the bushes, and dodging between the children's attempts at catching them. I'm entranced by the energy the Chittle's have. It doesn't look easy to have such speed and endurance with such short legs and big feet.

Just as I think that, a chittle trips over as a small boy follows. Aiden's attention is quickly caught. He attends to them both, comforting them and making sure they're both fine. My thoughts of his heartless nature quickly deteriorate in front of my eyes as I watch him getting up and bringing them both back on to their feet.

He notices me watching him. Instantly, I step back from the window and retreat back towards our room. Walking back, I'm processing what I had just seen, unable to wipe the smile from my face and calm the warmth swelling in my chest.

I turn the corner to the corridor our room is down, when I find myself a bit faint, and try to catch my footing as the walls begin to sway. A wave washes over me, clouding my head completely.

Falling to my knees, I'm overcome with a massive pain that shoots through my head, forcing a scream from my lips. Holding my head, I curl up on the floor, forcing my head to my knees as the pain grows.

A soft song rings through my head and a sweet voice begins to sing.

'Hush now, sweet child of time, flowers will bloom and die, for you my sweet child, time stands still, when you fly on the wings of a butterfly.

When all seems lost, you will always be found, let your light lead the way. As the years tick by, the birds will sing and fly, my promise to you, I will love you until the end of time.'

Her soft sweet voice soothes me as she holds me in her arms, her blue eyes bright with love. Her golden hair brushes my cheek as she rocks me by the window.

I watch her happily as she sings to me, making me forget why I was upset. I nestle in tighter to her, my most favorite place to be, as she sings my favorite song, sung only for me.

The sound of someone coming up the hall stops my mother's song and a man I don't recognize comes through the door.

My mother turns to see who has just entered; she freezes when she sees him.

My mother gasps. "What are you doing here?"

"That's the first thing you say to me after all these years?"

"How did you get in here? How did you get through the barrier?"

"It wasn't too hard with the right connections," he replies lazily.

"What do you want?"

"I have come for the child," he replies smoothly.

A cruel smile spreads across his face. Panic and confusion crash over me. He steps closer, pulling a dagger from his belt. She holds me tighter, as she stands abruptly, and retreats against the wall.

"No, you can't have her! I'll never allow it. How could you do this? We were family!" she yells, her voice cracking.

"Family! Oh, my, that is rich coming from you. I lost everything because of you. Now knowing what that child means, I'm only happy to return the favor."

"I don't know what you think I did, but you are seriously mistaken."

He laughs. "Either you don't know, or you are a great liar, since I was told you got a castle and crown for what you did to me, and here you are. I'm going to go with liar!" he hisses.

"You're wrong, this was my price to save you all!"

"Some price!" he yells back, venom dripping from his words.

"She has nothing to do with any of this. Leave her out of it!"

"You know what her existence means, and yet, you refuse to understand her importance, that alone shows she must come with me," he replies.

Panic and anger cross her face as she throws out a hand, the ring on her finger producing a barrier that holds him back.

"Oh, that won't save you when I have this," he chuckles shaking the dagger at her as it starts to glow.

Her eyes grow wide. Quickly, she turns to the window and jumps, holding me tight against her chest. Blue light traces around us, slowing our descent to the grass below.

The moment her feet touch the ground, she runs across the courtyard, past the fountain, to the maze hedges. I look over her shoulder as she runs. I see the strange man surfing the air on a blanket of blue light toward us.

A bolt of light shoots through the air and hits my mother in the back, hard, throwing us both to the ground. I scramble to my feet, rushing to my mother's side. Tears begin to fall. The man's dagger sparkles mockingly at me, embedded to the hilt in my mother's lifeless body.

"Mum! Please get up, please!" I shake her with my small hands, trying to get a response, tears streaming down my cheeks.

I back away as he moves closer.

"She thought she could hide you, but she never did learn not to trust so easily. That shows just how foolish she was," he laughs.

"What a shame! Ah, well, we couldn't have you getting in the way anymore, now could we?" he says towering over her body. Examining her, he nudges his boot into her side before laughing. "All you did to keep the child from her fate, and you end up like this. Oh, and the look on your face was priceless when you realized it was me this whole time."

He turns his attention to me. "Come, child," he commands.

I don't move.

"COME!" he bellows louder.

Still, I don't move.

He rips the dagger from my mother, and with one movement of his hand I'm pulled to him, my throat locked in his grip.

"No more games," he snarls. "You have a stubborn streak in you just like your mother. It will be so much fun squeezing that out of you," he says tightening his grip. "Are you going to behave?" he asks, sweetly this time.

I nod as best as I can.
He sets me down, holds out his hand, and I take it without a word. He smiles. "Good girl, call me Uncle. Your mother said it herself, we

are family." An evil smile spreads across his face while laughter fills the space as we walk.

I bolt upright in a cold sweat, breathing so hard it stings my throat. An arm shoots out at me, pulling me back against a hard surface. Another hand reaches around to pat my hair.

"Shh, it's okay, nothing's going to hurt you, I promise. Shh." It's Aiden's voice I hear, soft against my ear.

He plants a soft kiss in my hair, and I relax immediately into his arms. My breathing slowly returns to normal. His touch is comforting, making me feel safe and protected.

After a while, Aiden goes to pull away from me. The sudden disconnection sends me into a panic, and I grab his arms to hold me again.

"Please don't, not yet," I beg a little confused at my sudden outburst. "I know it can't be easy for you to comfort me like this but... please, a little longer."

He pauses for a moment, then I feel his arms snake around me again.

"Thank you," I whisper into his arm.

"You don't have to tell me, but I would be willing to listen if you want to talk," he says finally. "Shortly after you left the garden window, we heard screams from the hall, and when we ran to find where it was coming from, the guards and I found you curled up on the floor screaming. I brought you in here and had our healer called, but he could not find anything wrong with you."

But Aiden stayed to watch over me, and now he's comforting me. I curl my arms around his tighter.

"What happened?" he asks, as he continues to pat my hair.

"I think it was a memory," I say quietly.

"A bad one I would assume," he says gently.

"You could say that. I was ten, I think. My mother was singing to me by a window, I remember her eyes and hair, even her voice, she seemed so familiar, but I just can't make out her face clearly."

I tell him everything as he pulls my tear sodden face into his chest. "A strange man used a dagger to kill my mother, it was the same one I summoned when that beast attacked my family," I sob louder. "I knew I had seen it before...I'm sorry," I whimper as I notice my tears soaking his shirt.

"It can't be helped," he replies, continuing to stroke my hair, letting me cry until I have no tears left.

7

The Ball

The following morning, Angela knocks on the door.

"Prince Aiden? Are you coming to breakfast this morning?" she calls through the door.

My heart aches a little that I'm still not being acknowledged. I sigh. Aiden stirs and absentmindedly runs his fingers up and down my arm.

I don't need to open my eyes to know I found my way into his arms again. I slowly open my eyes and look up at a tired-looking Aiden. Did he stay up all night? He's looking down at me.

"Are you feeling good enough to go to breakfast?" he asks me gently.

I nod, slowly sitting up. I rub my swollen face.

"We will be right there," he calls back to Angela.

"Very good," she replies and leaves.

"I must look a right mess," I sigh.

He smiles warmly. "No worse than usual." he replies.

"Great, that makes me feel so much better," I playfully retort, swatting at him.

He laughs, catching my hand as I go to bat him again. His eyes lock on mine and I feel a familiar pull. He leans in slowly. I can feel his breath so close to mine, as he leans in closer, his eyes shift. Aiden quickly pulls back, clearing his throat as he jumps up and starts dressing. He's ready and out the door before I even get out of the bed.

I thought... I shake my head at my stupidity. Thought what? That maybe he wanted me as much as I want him? No, I don't want him, he's just confusing me with his kindness when we are alone, and I'm so starved for any kindness it is making me think something is there, that clearly is not.

Entering the hall for breakfast, I see Aiden notice me and scramble to his feet, leaving his plate barely touched.

"Are we in a rush to get to training today?" I ask, knowing full well this isn't the case.

"Training is cancelled today, there are too many preparations for tonight's celebration, and I have a lot to do. I don't care what you do today, just don't get in the way and don't cause me any trouble," he says harshly.

Great, and he's back to being an ass, I think, as I watch him leave the room. I sit at the table balancing a knife on its tip, absent-mindedly, when a plate of egg, toast and meat is shoved in front of me.

By the time I look up, I only see the servers back disappearing into the kitchen. I sigh. The room is empty as I eat, the silence deafening, and the overwhelming loneliness creeps in.

I'm startled when I feel something rub across my chin. It's my deerling! Nestling its body against my cheek, it tries to keep balanced on my shoulder. I'm still gaping at it when it starts to wander, and leaps from my shoulder to the fruit bowl toppling it over.

Apples, oranges, and some other fruits I have no idea what they are, scatter. The deerling gets up, shakes itself off, and chases after some grape like fruits, playing with them as a cat would a ball of twine.

I giggle as I watch it play, my mood lightening.

"Where did you come from?" I say mostly to myself.

I hadn't done the summons for it to be here. I look around the room again, and still don't see anyone. I'm certain no one will come in while they know I'm here. I reach into my bag and pull out my book. I look through the book from cover to cover, to find something on how it could be summoned without me calling it until I reach the back of the book.

Teleportation, this is exceedingly difficult magic and can only be attempted after hand movement is no longer required, as teleportation is one of the hardest spells to use. It is a matter of body and mind as one. You must know your magic to the point that you can feel it in all you do.

"Hm, so as I get stronger, it's more of becoming one with your magic. It's a state of mind, a feeling. This is it! My way home!" I squeal Excitedly, *I swear this was not in the book before,* I shake my head, pushing the thought from my mind, I read the directions over and over, trying to start with something simple like moving one of the grape things the deerling is playing with, but nothing happens.

I try calling a candle at the end of the banquet table, but nothing. I try imagining myself in the chair three down from me, but still nothing. *I guess I'm not as in touch with my magic as I thought I might be,* I sigh.

I leave the hall to go to the bloom tree for the rest of the day and practice my book without using my hands, and surprisingly, I do much better than I thought I would. As the light begins to fade, a chittle bursts out of the long grass and rolls over onto its feet from the abrupt stop.

I jump in surprise at the sudden appearance. Collecting myself, I lean down to help it up, and it greets me happily with clicks and cute little pop sounds it makes in its cheeks. I assume it's grateful for my help.

Excitedly, it seems to remember what it was there to do and pulls a folded piece of paper from its back, handing it to me. I take it and give a smile.

"Thank you," I say.

Happy with itself, the chittle turns and disappears back into the long grass.

I open the letter. It's from Aiden.

Come back now, it's time to get ready, everything has been arranged and is waiting for you in our room, don't leave me waiting and don't make me come after you.
Aiden.
I sigh, pack up my things, and leave, not wanting to know what he will do if I try to play hooky on this ball.

When I get back, as he said, there is a beautiful floor-length dress of ivory silk, and dusted with what looks like diamond powder, giving the dress an exquisite sparkle. The sleeves are short, and sit off the shoulders, and the front of the bodice has a netting of jewels.

A knock sounds at the door and Madeleine enters the room.

I beam at her. "Madeline! What are you doing here?" I ask her.

"I've come to help you get into your dress for the ceremonial ball. The others thought sending me was a punishment," she laughs then catches herself. "Oh, I'm sorry I didn't mean..." she starts to say.

"It's okay, I understand. How about we not let them know otherwise," I say with a laugh.

She smiles back at me, relieved. "Absolutely, come on let's get you ready," she says excitedly.

"You said ceremonial ball" I say thinking back on her words, "Is this the ceremony everyone has been going on about?"

"Yes, didn't you get told?" she asks.

No, I didn't, I was only told I had to be ready to host a ball with Aiden.

"Yes, well that is what this is, you are both hosting the ball as a couple announcing your unity" she replies happily.

I'm a little relieved the ceremony wasn't what I was expecting.

I'm so glad I had Madeleine to help me into this damn dress.

Although it's beautiful, it's so tight I can hardly breathe in it. How I wish I was still in my room with Madeline talking and laughing.

Still our time together really cheered me up enough to get me through this catastrophe waiting to happen, although with all the hard work Aiden put into this, I want everything to go right for him, so I smile and greet as I'm told.

This celebration is a massive event. The hall is bustling with hundreds of guests of all different races. I gape as I realize why the ballroom has such high ceilings, it's for the guests that are as tall as a house to attend. The floor pounds under my feet as a huge rock creature moves towards us, lowers his massive head down in greeting to Aidan at my side, then steps over us with one step. I follow him with my gaze through the giant doors to the ballroom, my mouth still a gape.

"Close your mouth," Aiden scolds in a whisper so only I can hear.

He greets our next guests, a lovely couple with long legs and thin green bodies. Both have their suit and dress made of moss, vines and flowers. I look at the woman. She is stunning, her hair is autumn leaves that cascade down her back and shoulders. She has a beautiful crystal tiara placed on her head. Her dress is long, and flows behind her, trimmed with Incredible flowers and luscious green vines that cross over her chest and around her waist, and fall at a split in the front of her dress that shows her long slender legs. Her shoes are a green jade.

We stand at the entrance for a couple of hours, just meeting and greeting guests from all across the land. I am delighted with everything I see and learn, soaking everything in. There are guests that look like a dragon and a snake got together, and others that are small and slimy, like snails merged with a penguin. There are even guests that look like a troll and a Muppet started a family.

Aiden had to scold me so many times, and remind me to control myself as my enthusiasm was too much. But as much as he scolds me, I've seen a smirk appear in the corners of his mouth after each time.

After all the greetings have been done, we enter the hall and Aiden escorts me around the room. We stop and have polite conversation, a few times we come across guests I don't understand and Aiden acts as a translator, taking a lot of pressure off of me. Everyone has been very pleasant to me so far and not at all as I had imagined they would be. The night is going well and I've had a dare, I say it? A good time, just as the thought crosses my mind, a large crash booms through the room.

"What on earth was that?" I ask Aiden.

"It sounds like it came from the kitchen. I'll go investigate. You stay here," he says, and leaves quickly.

Everyone is bunched up close in the room. The music has started up again from Aiden's orders, but he still has not returned. I assume it's not life-threatening, but it is still a problem. The room is full of tall guests, and I find myself lost now Aiden is not at my side.

A woman about the same age as me knocks into me, a little too hard for it to have been an accident, and I fall backwards, tripping on my dress.

"Don't expect me to apologize," she says venomously, crossing her arms.

"I don't expect anything. I'm sure it would not have happened if I was paying attention," I reply, trying to defuse the situation as guests surround us, wanting to see what all the commotion is all about.

"Don't give us that, the only good vermillion is a dead one," I hear another voice say.

I get up and brush my dress off trying to hold back the tears threatening my eyes. *Aiden, where are you?* I think as I search the room for him.

"I'm sorry you feel that way, but I'm not them. I don't know what you have been through, but I'm not my people and I'm not my father, I'm *me*," I say with as much strength as I can muster. The group around me presses in on me, giving me less and less space to breathe. "Now, please, let me pass," I ask, having enough of this increasingly uncomfortable evening.

"You really think you have any right to demand anything from us? You should be grateful you're not dead yet. You should be kissing our shoes with gratitude," another says with a laugh.

I look around, trying desperately to find Aiden. *Where is he?* Aiden wouldn't allow this. Breathing is getting harder, and I can't stop the desperate need to get away from them from taking over me.

Everyone gasps, and steps back slightly. There's an uproar of chatter. My deerling is sitting on the floor just in front of my toes, but it does not look impressed. I hear the chatter get louder and comments reach my ears.

"Oh my God! I can't believe she has the audacity to show off her magic here," someone whispers.

The guests get louder and begin pressing in on us, anger spreading across their faces. My deerling steps forward, and in a huge burst of light, grows in size, effectively forcing the group back.

My deerling is now in a protective stance. With every angry gaze on me, I wish so deeply I was anywhere but here. I grab my head as a shock runs through my body and light blinds me. When I open my eyes, I find myself on the grass under the night sky. My eyes adjust, and I realize the dazzling lights above me are not stars, but the flowers of the bloom tree.

I look up in awe as I take in the sight before me. I've never seen it at night, I've always been back in the castle before dark. The tree's flowers shine with beautiful twinkling lights.

Oh my God! I just teleported here! My excitement fills me at my accomplishment, but quickly fades as I think of how angry it would have made everyone else. I flop on the grass, my arms outstretched. No matter what I do, I just can't win.

I don't move for a long while, but after a time I make my way back to the castle, hoping the ball is over and everyone has gone by now. I'm lucky to find everyone has left and the castle is quiet. I pass a door just down the hall from our bedroom, where I hear Aiden's voice.

"She doesn't know how to help herself does she? With everything going on and the delicate position she's in, you would think she would be more careful. She is undisciplined, careless, clueless, and has a great disregard for safety. She was making progress, and then I leave her for a few moments and all hell breaks loose," I hear Aiden say in an angry voice.

"Why wasn't she with you? It's your job to keep her out of trouble. She knows very little of this place, our ways, and our people, and is still learning to control her powers!" his father bellows, their voices competing in volume.

"Don't give me that. How can I do anything if I'm always spending my time cleaning up after her screw-ups?" he shouts back.

"She wouldn't screw up if you were keeping an eye on her instead of avoiding her until she messes up!" the king yells.

"I wasn't avoiding her. There was an incident in the kitchen, it was chaos," Aiden grumbles.

"Don't give me that. You got a chance to get away and you took it, leaving her to the wolves!" he shouts.

"Fine, I can't stand being around her. Is that what you want to hear? I can't understand how you can defend her when all you ever wanted was to lead her kind to be slaughtered, since they're the reason mother is dead! What changed?" Aiden asks angrily.

8

Going Home

I gasp. Aiden lost his mum because of my family? My heart breaks and the tears fall. *No wonder he can't bring himself to feel anything for me,* I cry. I can't stay here any longer.

I need to go. I never realized how much pain I was causing him. I thought I could change his mind about me, but all I did was make a bad thing worse for him. My tears fall heavier as I make it back to our room.

I think my going back home will be best for everyone, especially Aiden. Madeline is my only friend here, and I'm sure she will be better off without me, too. If not for me, I believe she wouldn't be treated so badly. I've made up my mind. Light magic has no known limitations, if I can move myself from here to the bloom tree, I can send myself home.

I did it in the ballroom, I know how it felt. I was connected to my power. I could feel it coursing through my veins. I remember the feeling as I picture my sister's home firmly in my mind. I concentrate, pushing everything else out. Light magic begins to form around me and I feel it.

Aiden enters the room the moment the familiar light blinds me forcing my eyes to close, I'm finally going home.

I slowly open my eyes as the light fades away. I'm in my sister's house. My heart leaps for joy. I take in every detail. I can't contain my delight. It's dark outside. I pass the grandfather clock in the hall, it's two am. Everyone will be asleep in bed.

This clock was once our parent's prized possession, passed down from generation to generation. I run my hands down its woodwork, the thought of the carvings back home spring to mind. The thought is uninviting as it makes me think of Aiden...

I make my way up the stairs carefully, not wanting to wake my niece and nephew. I open the door, to selfish to pass up giving them a kiss on their little cheeks. Chris and Mira don't stir, and I'm grateful. I quietly make my way to Tom and Mia's room.

Quietly as I can, I open the door. It squeaks as it opens. Tom and Mia are lying in bed sound asleep. I notice there is distance between them. With how much they paw over each other, I figured they would be glued together in their sleep, too.

Aiden and I, no matter how hard we fight it, no matter how angry we are at each other, or what barriers we put between us, they're all torn down through the night and we find ourselves wrapped around each other every morning.

Pushing the thought away, I lean down and push a loose strand of hair behind Mia's ear, caressing my thumb against her cheek. She stirs, opening her eyes slightly, then a little more. I smile down at her, but she doesn't smile back.

Oh... Is she mad at me for waking her up...? Or for what happened in the park? Or maybe because I disappeared?

After a while, Mia sighs and sits up. She reaches over to her bedside table and picks up a picture of Mia and I at her hen's party. I look at it, too.

My smile reappears, spreading across my face. We are each holding a wine glass up to the camera with one hand, as we make a crude gesture, sticking our tongues between our two spread fingers. That night was insane. I remember the male strippers we did tequila shots off in the middle of the club. That night they let us do whatever we wanted.

The memory makes me giggle. Suddenly, Mia's head snaps away from the picture and looks in my direction, but seems to be looking through me.

Oh no... the realization hits me hard, a lump forming in my throat. She can't see me.

"Is there anyone there?" she calls.

Tears start to prickle at my eyes, but I force them back, not sure how to handle this now. I know she can still hear me, as my giggle startled her. I take a deep breath, realizing what I must do now.

"Yes, Mia it's me," I whisper.

Startled, she straightens up more, looking out around the room. "Bree?" she asks.

"Yes, I'm here next to you," I answer.

"Why can't I see you?" She covers her mouth, eyes wide. "Oh my God, are you dead?" She starts to cry.

"No, no, no, I'm not dead at all," I say, trying to comfort her.

She abruptly stops crying. A new look of confusion crosses her face. "Then why can't I see you?" she asks.

"Good question, but I think I know why. You remember the day at the park?" I ask her.

"How can I forget? What I saw that day was my sister staring at something no one else could see, then being tossed and sliced in front of her family, then disappearing before our eyes," she says crossing her arms.

"I'm sorry," I say glumly. "Well, I saw a creature not of this world called an Akuma. It attacked us, and somehow, I teleported it back home. I found my birth parents are from there, the same as me," I say solemnly. "I didn't realize the more I trained my light magic to get back to you, the less of this world I would become, which is why I believe you can't see me. In time, you probably won't be able to hear me either."

The thought brings tears to my eyes. Mia smiles and leans forward in my direction.

"This place was never for you. It makes sense you would find your way back there, and if it's us you're worried about, don't. Just knowing you're alive and safe brings me such joy and relief you can't imagine," she says.

I wipe the tears away and smile back, even though she can't see me. "You are accepting this far better than I thought you would," I confess.

"After all I have seen and been through lately, nothing surprises me," Mia admits.

"I hope you know how much I love you," I say, with every bit of feeling I have.

"If it's anything like me, then I sure do," she replies in kind.

We spend the rest of the night talking about everything that's gone on in the last few months, and as the light starts to peek through the windows, I know I have to go before the others awake so I don't cause any questions or problems for Mia. I hold her tight to me, forming a memory of her in this moment.

"I love you so much," I whimper into her auburn hair.

"And I love you," she sniffles. "You go back there and show them you belong, and anything you do will be great and beautiful."

We hold each other tight as we say our final goodbyes.

9

As One

The light fades and my vision comes back. Aiden is sitting on the bed carving a long wooden chain. He doesn't look up, keeping his attention on the chain-link he is smoothing out.

"You knew, didn't you?" I ask.

"That they wouldn't see you? That you couldn't stay there? Yeah, I did, but you never would have taken my word for it. I guess it's one of those things you need to learn for yourself. Our magic can't stay in that world for long, depending on how you go there, depends on the time limit, and even your great and powerful light magic can't stay there," he says.

"What do you mean? There's another way?" I ask.

"Of course, how do you think you got there in the first place and managed to stay for the last seventeen years? Though, I doubt you could do it again for anywhere near that long, if at all," he says, casually with a shrug.

"You knew I wanted to go back home. Why would you keep this from me, if it gets rid of me? I know that's what you want more than anything!" I shout a little louder than I intend.

He drops his chain resting it in his lap, and leans forward. "Don't speak of things you know nothing about," he hisses at me.

"How can you say that to me? Every chance you get, you taunt me or ignore me. I don't know what I ever did to make you hate me so much, but for me...." I think for a moment about how I want to say this. "I don't hate you at all, Aiden. I have tried but I just don't, even when you are being your usual ass self."

He cocks an eyebrow at me for calling him an ass, but doesn't say anything so I continue.

"The way you are with your people, the way you are with the creatures you interact with, I just wish you would be that way with...*me*," I admit in almost a whisper, lowering my head to look at my hands. "You always found a way to surprise me just as I am done with how rotten you are to me. You show a glimpse of your soft side and I just can't be mad."

He seems amused by my words, since I am holding my heart out to him It is starting to annoy me, but still he stays quiet.

"Aiden! I am bearing my heart out to you, can you please stop? Is this a big joke to you?!" I ask angrily.

"Don't say that, I'm listening to you," Aiden bites back.

"Every word I say, you are looking at me like I'm being stupid."

"Not once did I say that!" he argues back.

"This is always how all our conversations go. I thought this time it would be a little more civil!" I throw back at him in a huff.

Bringing the decibels of the argument back down he asks, "Then why did you try to run away?"

"I overheard the conversation you were having with your father in his study. No matter how I felt, I figured you would be happier if I was gone," I say honestly.

He runs his hand through his black hair, exasperated. "That's why you left?" he asks. "That's not what you think it was," he says shaking his head.

I cross my arms. "Then explain how I misheard you," I snap.

"Oh, I'm not saying you misheard me, I'm saying it's not what you think," he retorts.

I snap again, "How is that any different?"

He says nothing.

"If there is another way for me to go home, tell me, and I won't be a problem for you anymore," I say quietly.

Jumping to his feet he bellows at me, "Do you really want to run away from me that badly? Do you really remember NOTHING AT ALL?"

"Remember what?" I reply, shocked.

He exhales. "Nothing, forget it," he says, completely defused.

I snap again growling "No, I won't. What did you mean by that?"

He turns his gaze from mine, running his hands through his hair again. I don't know what to say to him. What does he want from me?

Frustrated, he throws his hands down at his side, fists clenched, and storms over to where I'm standing. He stops right in front of me and he looks at me for a moment. "You need to stop jumping to conclusions," he says sharply. He grabs my face, pinning it between his hands, and kisses me hard.

His sudden assault takes me by surprise. I feel his need for me in the desperation of his kiss. As my mind has gone blank. I realize my need for him, too.

I raise my shaking hands to his shoulders, gliding them up and around him, deepening our kiss. His right-hand slides down my face, to my neck, over my shoulder, and down my back. He wraps his arms around my waist, pulling me tight against him, as his tongue invades my mouth.

My head is light, filled with nothing but him as the sensations burn through my body. I tighten my grip around his neck, sliding my left hand down his back. He walks forward, pushing me backward until I feel the bed at the back of my legs. Slowly, he lowers me down onto the bed, not taking his mouth from mine.

We are holding each other so tightly needing more than our bodies will allow, we are so lost in each other that we don't notice our magic leaving us.

It hovers above our intertwined forms, Purple and Blue blend together like a colorful mist shimmering above us. It pulses brighter and brighter sparkling like diamonds, our mist of color explodes, raining down on us in an explosive fireworks display.

10

Crystal Cave

"Bree! Bree! Quick wake up we have to go!"

I wake up, a young boy of around 14, is pulling my blankets off me, forcing me to get out of bed.

"What's going on?" I ask.

"Shh, quiet," he says holding a finger to my mouth.

"Quick get dressed we have to go, now," he says in a whisper.

I get dressed quickly and quietly. Once I'm ready, he grabs my hand.

"No magic or they will see," he whispers.

"Okay," I say, groggy and very confused.

It's not the first time he's done things like this in the middle of the night, but he's never been so forceful. He's worried about something.

He leads me out my bedroom window, the way he came in. It's so high I let out a gasp as I look down.

"Shh, don't look down. Don't look anywhere but at me, okay?" He looks straight into my eyes and I calm a little. Without a word, I nod at him so he knows I'm fine now.

We sidestep around the shallow ledge to the side of the castle where a large tree stands. The boy grabs one of the large branches and pulls himself up into the tree. He holds out a hand to me.

"Quick, before the guards come back round," he says quietly.

I'm so scared. It's so high, and he's so much taller than I am. I lean back against the wall. The boy reaches out to me a little further.

"Bree, trust me. I will never let anything happen to you, I swear on my life," his look imploring, maybe even desperate.

All fear gone, I leap. He catches me and pulls me into the tree. We make our way down the thick branches to the bottom. The boy jumps to the ground for the last part, holding out his arms for me to do the same. Without hesitation, I drop into his arms. He quickly looks around and dashes off towards the trees in the distance, dragging me along with him. Lights start appearing behind us as I hear a voice calling out. They know I'm missing.

"Quickly, we need to run faster," he implores.

I pick up my pace, trying my best to match his. The trees are getting closer and closer the deeper we go into the woods. Branches are flying past us, scratching at my face, arms, and legs, but I ignore the pain and keep running. We have been running for a while now, my breath is burning in my throat.

"Please, I can't keep this up for much longer," I implore him.

"Just a little further," he says, not slowing his pace or taking his eyes off where he's going.

We come up to a large mound and the boy slows down. He lets go of my hand and disappears behind a curtain of vines with glowing flowers that dot the surface. The vines are lighting the area so gently. He returns, grabbing my hand once again and reefing me behind the curtain of vines with him. They arch away from the wall, giving us room to walk around without being seen. A little way up a purple light appears getting brighter and brighter.

He stops in front of a door made of purple light with ancient markings. He holds out his hand and presses it to the door. In a burst of light, it dissipates, revealing a tunnel. Once we step inside, the door reappears behind us, glowing brightly again.

"Where are we going?" I ask, as he pulls me further and further through the tunnels.

"You will see, we are almost there," he says smiling at me.

We keep walking until light begins to flood the tunnel. He stops abruptly, forcing me to bump into him, stepping out into a wide-open cave deep within the mountain.

I look around in awe as he guides me in. A soft moss carpets the ground under my feet, surrounding a large lake of a magnificent clear blue. The water lights up the entire cave. It's like a mirror reflecting the brilliant colors of the impressive gems littering the walls.

"This is the most beautiful place I have ever seen," I say in awe.

A smile appears on his face. "I have always wanted to bring you here," he confesses.

"And now you have." I smile back at him, placing my free hand over his hand that is holding my other hand captive. His smile disappears.

"What's wrong." I ask.

"It's nothing, don't worry. I just want to enjoy this time I have with you."

I squeeze his hand tight, pressing my cheek into his shoulder as we walk side by side. At the end of the lake the ground disappears. A large, curved staircase comes into view.

As we descend, I notice ancient stones lining the stairs all the way down. He notices my curiosity, and a smile returns to his face again.

"This is a secret cavern that has been entrusted to my family for hundreds of years to protect. Here is where they say all magic was born. Over the years it was forgotten about, and only the king and the future king were ever told of its existence," the boy divulges.

I look at him in shock, my mouth wide. "We are going to get into such trouble if they find out you brought me here," I whisper.

His smile widens, stopping on the stair below to face me.

"I don't ever want to hold any secrets from you. I don't want to worry about our families finding out about us or the wars between the kingdoms, all I want to worry about is keeping you safe," he states firmly. more like a man than the young boy I have grown to love. He rests his forehead against mine, holding both my hands in his."I will never marry, unless it's you, for wherever you go, my heart goes with you," he says gently.

"You're scaring me. What's wrong?" I ask, nestling my nose to his.

"I love you and I always will. One day all this will be over, and by that time we will be old enough to wed. From now until the end of time, I will always be yours," he proclaims.

My heart swells at his words, drowning in love for him. "And I will always be yours." I say.

He gently brushes a kiss to my cheek giving my hands a squeeze. He turns from me, releasing one of my hands, and continues down the stairs. I don't know what's wrong, or what I could say to him to make whatever he's feeling go away. I choose to stay quiet as we continue down.

We finally reach the bottom, where a rock pool sits. Shimmering wisps of magic dance around the water below like graceful fish. A large stone tablet stands proud behind it with ancient markings I can't understand.

I turn back to look at the stairs and see they circle the whole room like seats. The rock pool is the object of interest. The boy sits on the edge of the pool, and gently skim's his palm across the water. He retracts his hand quickly.

The water begins to move as the wisps start diving in and out of the water in a beautiful display of color. He stands, grabbing my hands.

"We're out of time," he says, pressing his head to mine.

"We have all the time in the world," I reply.

He looks at me, wrapping his arms around my waist. He steps forward, pushing me back. He stops, raising one hand to my cheek. "I will never stop loving you, and I will do anything to protect you, even if you can't be at my side," he says with such sadness.

"What is going on? Tell me, please!" I say, caressing his hand on my cheek with mine.

"You're in danger, Bree, and there is no way I'm letting them have you," he states.

I go to say something in argument, but he jolts forward, kissing me hard. A powerful surge bolts through me. Our magic is bursting to life around us, weaving together as one.

I can feel his desperation and yearning in his kiss. A tear hits my cheek. I open my eyes and see he's crying. He pushes me away from him sharply, abruptly breaking our connection. I fall backward, landing into the rock pool. The wisps wrap around me, dragging me down to its deepest depths. His face disappears from my view. I kick and flail desperately, trying to reach him, but soon everything disappears.

"AIDEN!" I scream.

I I

The Day It All Fell

I fly up, calling out. My heart racing a million miles, beads of sweat dripping from my body, trying desperately to catch my breath. Aiden bolts upright, throwing his arms around me.

"Shh, shh, shh," he says, trying to soothe me.

"It's just a dream, it's just a dream. I'm here, nothing's ever going to hurt you while I'm around," he says soothingly.

I manage to calm down enough to notice it's the middle of the night, and I'm safe and sound in our bed. "It's just a dream? But it felt so real," I say in disbelief.

"Everything is okay now," Aiden says, holding me tightly.

"Aiden?" I say, my voice muffled in his chest.

"Yes?" he replies.

"Did we know each other as kids?"

Aiden tightens his hold on me, pulling me closer.

"Did you remember something?" he asks softly, not letting me go.

"My dream, it was so real. I have been having short dreams of the same dark-haired boy. He would be teasing me in one dream, then getting a bird to give me a flower the next. And this time it was so detailed. In this one, I'm about twelve. There was a mirror lake. I could feel the moss under my feet, and there were steps down to an ancient pool full of magical wisps that danced over the water," I say in a rush.

Aiden is shaking slightly. His breathing is heavier. His hold on me is tighter than before, listening to me intently. "Was there more?" he asks in a cracked voice.

"Yes," I reply.

Aiden buries his head into my shoulder waiting for what I say next.

"The boy touched the water, stirring up the wisps, he walked me to the edge of the pool and gave me my first kiss, then pushed me in. Why are all my dreams filled with him? And why do I feel like that boy was you?" I say in a muffled voice from the curve in his neck.

"That's because it was me," he says quietly.

"YOU PUSHED ME!" I yell, as I poke him in the chest with a forceful finger. He winces but does not stop me. "You've been waiting all this time for me to remember you?" I ask.

He nods lightly but doesn't say anything.

"The pool where you pushed me in, that's how I got to the other world where Mia found me, wasn't it?" I ask.

He nods again.

"That was the other way you were talking about, then. I assume that the pool stripped me of my memories and powers, which was how I was able to stay there for so long, and you were saying something about a time limit. My time was up the day I had my first vision of you because straight after the Akuma attacked me, I wound up back here. Why didn't you tell me?"

Aiden looks at me for a few moments, then sighs.

"Fear that without your memories the life you led there without me was better for you... safer," He lowers his eyes. "My desire to keep you safe drove you from me, then once I had you back, all you wanted was the life back that I pushed you into," he adds.

"Literally," I say with a smirk.

Aiden scowls at me, but continues. "I didn't feel I had the right to take that from you, too, and once you remembered what I had done, I thought it would drive you away from me anyway. Not to mention, the more you became a part of this place the harder it would be to find your way back." He exhales. "Unsure of what you remember, I couldn't just tell you, 'hey we have been in love since we were kids.' How could I know if you still felt the same way you did back then? It's been seventeen years, Bree," he says.

"So, are you saying you love me?" I ask in a hum, slowly leaning into him. "Did you ever stop loving me?" I ask, running a hand through his hair.

He closes his eyes at my touch. "Yes, Bree, I love you and I have never, not for a single moment, stopped loving you," he answers cupping his hand over mine.

"The first time I saw you in San Diego was in a day dream," I murmur.

"What day dream?" he asks. "Is this why you were afraid of me when you first arrived?"

I explain my daydream and Aiden listens intently.

"That was no dream, it really happened. That happened the day we went to Varillia. Your father was threatening all the kingdoms, saying that if you were not returned to him, he would destroy everyone throughout all the lands. All the kingdoms came together in one big battle to destroy him and his people once and for all. The battle went on for years, and in the end, Verillia fell, and burned to the ground. On the final day, I faced your father just as you saw," Aiden says.

"So that was my father fighting you?" I ask.

"Yes," he answers.

"I have so many questions," I say, overwhelmed.

"I'm sure you do, but right now I think it's time to rest. We can talk more in the morning, or if you're too full of energy to sleep I can think of a way to put that energy to good use," he says, brushing my hair off my shoulder. He starts planting little kisses down my neck.

"You're trying to distract me," I say weakly.

"Yep, is it working?" he asks coyly, as he continues his gentle assault.

A moan escapes my lips as he brushes that damn spot right below my ear and I lose it, forgetting everything, I let him take me away to sheer bliss.

I open my eyes the following morning and find Aiden awake before me, his head resting in his hand as he watches me sleep. He greets me with a broad smile, lowers his head, and kisses me sweetly.

"Good morning," he says with a bright smile.

"Good morning," I beam back.

Aiden pushes an arm under me, pulling me into him.

"Mmm, I like it here," I say, as I nestle my face into his chest.

"I like it here, too," he says, squeezing me slightly.

We lay in each other's embrace, his chin resting on the crown of my head as I absentmindedly run my thumb up and down one of his arms that holds me to him. He presses a soft kiss in my hair.

"What are you thinking?" he asks.

"What just happened," I reply.

"Me too," his grin spreading through my hair.

I smile and pull at a small tuft of hair on his arm. "I didn't mean that." I giggle.

"Ow," he laughs.

"I mean I feel different. I mean we made a bond when you first touched me when I first arrived, but that's not right, is it?" I ask.

"No, it's not, because our real bond was made the day I kissed you in the crystal cave. I think our being together unlocked some things, but didn't relight until last night," he replies.

"But all that commotion about a bond, what was that?" I ask.

"Since a bond is so rare, not many know what a real bond is like. I think it was staged to keep you from being killed when you first arrived back here," he ponders.

"Staged? How?" I ask.

"The only magic that could possibly pull it off would be light magic. I thought you remembered me and made a scene to stay together, but from the way you acted I quickly realized if you didn't remember, and it wasn't you, then it had to come from someone else," Aiden replies.

"But then that would mean there is another with my magic. I thought all of my people perished," I answer.

"Exactly," he says back.

"I thought you had something to do with all this, but from what I understand from you now, it seems you're being played, too," he comments.

"What do you mean?" I ask.

"Well...you had a vision of me fighting your father, then straight after that an Akuma seeks you out, and you both drop on a table right in front of us. Then before anyone can say anything about you, a bond is made, locking you to me, ensuring your protection," he answers.

"The argument I overheard, and as you said, I jumped to the wrong conclusion?" I ask. "You only said what you said because you don't trust him, do you?"

"You're right, I don't, not since we came back from your homeland. He's been acting differently. At first it was small things. He stopped training and using magic. He started traveling a lot, but when you arrived, he was unusually loving to you and very distant to me. The family portraits came down and the tapestry went up," he replies.

"You think somehow he had something to do with the fake bond?" I ask.

"Yes, I do, but I don't understand how or why. Our fathers hated each other and everything the other stood for. I can't understand how he could be so calm about the whole thing." Aiden says. The thought pulls at my chest. "And I also believe whoever is behind all this, they never expected we would have such history," he grins.

"That's putting it lightly," I giggle.

"We will have to play along for the time being, until we know more about what's going on, but at least our newfound information has helped in leaps and bounds." He runs his hands down my sides. His mouth runs up the arch of my shoulder. "I'm just glad I didn't have to kill you," he says, amusement in his voice.

"Oh, really?" I laugh. "As if you ever could."

He flips me round to face him, and shoves me back. He pins me to the bed in one quick motion, my hands pinned beneath his. Aiden looks down at me, a smile on his face. He thinks for a moment.

"Your right I don't think I could." He lowers his head and kisses me softly.

I open my eyes when he pulls away. A lustful grin appears on his face as he nudges my legs apart. I bite my lower lip, trying to stop my smile from spreading but fail.

"But I can think of a few things I know I am capable of," he replies seductively.

I 2

The Garden

When I wake, I find Aiden is gone but a tray of breakfast and a note is left to greet me.

Had to leave early, didn't want to wake you, meet me in the garden when you're ready, love Aiden x.

I finish breakfast quickly. Even though I know it hasn't been long since we saw each other, I still can't wait to see him. I stroll out the doors to the garden. It's a lovely day. The sky is a beautiful blue, not a cloud in sight. The birds are singing in the trees, as butterflies flutter over the flowers.

I hold out my hand as one moves closer to me. It's breathtaking. The butterfly rests in my open palm. Its wings are bigger than my hand, with an assortment of colors pulsing and changing.

The sound of beating wings brings my attention back to my surroundings, to find the space I occupy is engulfed by a large variety of butterflies, big and small. It's like something from a dream.

I notice Aiden approaching me. I look over at him beaming, holding out my hands with the big butterfly still happily perched in my palm. He stills, a look of shock covers his face. My smile leaves me, replaced with concern.

"What's wrong?" I ask.

"Nothing's wrong per-say, it's more to the point of, how are you using creature magic?" he speculates.

"I'm what?" I gasp.

"You're surrounded by butterflies and you have a Starlite butterfly, the rarest of them all, perched in your hand. There is no other explanation," Aiden answers.

"Wow, a Starlite butterfly?" I ask, mesmerized.

"Yes," Aiden replies.

"Why are they so rare?" I ask, examining the exquisite colors pulsing and shimmering through its incredible wings.

"I don't know for sure, no one does. There are a lot of stories about them. Like you, they are a magnificent mystery," he replies fondly.

I smile back, then remember what we were just talking about. "Wait a minute, you were just saying I was using creature magic!" I exclaim. "But I thought this was you, like what you did when we were children," I say, confused.

"No Bree, I'm not doing this, you are," he corrects.

"Then if I'm using your magic doesn't that mean you can use mine?" I say, a little excited.

"I don't think so. It's unheard of for magic to be shared, but then again, light magic has very few things known about it except by those who wield it. Not to mention, it's never been bonded with another type of magic before either," he declares. "It could be that you have taken a bit of my magic or maybe you can imitate it now," he says, thoughtfully stroking his chin.

"It's not like I can call for a dagger and expect it to appear in my hand like you do," he says, holding out his hand.

"Well then, what do you call that?" I say, eyeing the dagger that is now in his hand. I smile broadly showing my teeth. "I knew it. Our magic has become one!" I squeal.

"It must be the bond," Aiden says, analyzing the dagger in shock.

"If this is the bond then why didn't this happen when it was first made?" I ask, confused.

"I don't believe a bond like this can be made as children; I think as our bond grows so do our abilities. Like I said before, we don't know what light magic is capable of and bonds are rare, let alone a light magic bond," Aiden says, still examining the blade in his hand. "Until we know for sure what's going on and who's behind all this, we need to be very careful how we act in public." Aiden stops talking for a moment and grabs my hand quickly. "We shouldn't talk here, let's go someplace safe. Come with me," Aiden says, jumping a little when the blade vanishes from his hand.

Shaking it off quickly, he leads me out of the garden and into the castle. He says nothing, he just leads me further down the halls to a stone staircase. It gets colder the deeper we go down, till we get to a large iron door. Aiden pulls out a bunch of old iron keys from his pocket, chooses one particularly old one, fits it into the door, and opens it. Inside it's cold, and dark and the air is old and stale. Once we step inside, Aiden closes the door behind us, engulfing us in complete darkness.

"Ahh... want to give us some light, Bree?" Aiden asks, patting me on the backside.

I squeak at the playful move. "Oh, Ah sure," I smile. I think of a light orb like the ones around the castle and one appears flooding the room with my blue light.

"That's perfect," he says, planting a soft kiss on my lips as he passes me.

The room is full of what looks like old family portraits, stacks of old books, scrolls, suits of armor, and very old weapons.

"This is an old storeroom. It's full of stuff from hundreds of years ago. Only my father and I have keys to this room, as it holds most of our old heritage," Aiden answers before I can even ask the question.

We pass chests of all shapes and sizes, stone busts of what I assume to be of previous royals, and large statues of gods and goddesses wearing nothing, or next to nothing. We keep walking deeper into the room.

"I used to come here a lot when I was a boy. I liked hiding in here to get away from my teachers and all the formalities. I liked coming here to be left alone. I built a fortress right at the back so I had time to hide if someone found me, but my mother would always find me here," he smiles as if recalling a sweet memory.

My shoulder brushes across something and it crashes to the stone floor, making me jump. "Oh, I'm so sorry." I say, a little panicked. I bend down to pick up the large portrait pile I just knocked over.

"That's alright, here, let me help," Aiden says soothingly.

All the portraits are pictures of Aiden at different ages. I run my fingers over one of him at age fourteen when I remembered him most clearly. Aiden notices my smile and rests his hand on mine. I snap out of our little moment, my attention trailing off to the two other people in the portrait.

The woman is a definite beauty, with hair of long golden waves. Her eyes are a magnificent blue and skin that looked like porcelain, so soft and delicate you would think she would shatter if you touched her, and beside her, a rather large man, much taller than her, his hair short and black, complimenting his strong features, He looks a lot like.... eyes wide, I look at Aiden.

"Aiden who is this?" I say, a little panicked.

"That's my father," he says, confused.

"I figured you would say that," I say, not taking my eyes off the portrait. "This is what you see when you look at your father?" I ask, looking at him this time, a serious look now appearing on my face.

"Yes," he replies cautiously.

I have his full attention now and he's worried. I don't blame him. I take a deep breath. "This is not who I see when I look at your father."

He's trying to process what I'm telling him. His hands are in his hair now. "My father has been acting strange ever since we came back from our attack on Varillia. I knew something was not right with him, that's why I have been playing it safe around him, keeping my cards close to my chest, so to speak." He starts pacing up and down now as he's processing and talking out loud. "From the moment we came back, it was as if I had done something that had made him furious with me. He didn't want to eat with me or do our usual training together or any-thing." His talking has sped up now. I thought it was especially strange when you turned up and the moment, he saw your eyes, he was as soft and accepting as anything, Oh my god, this all makes so much sense now!" He freezes on the spot and looks at me in horror. "If that's not my father then that means he's most likely dead." He drops to his knees.

I rush over to him and wrap my arms around his head, holding his face to my chest. I can only imagine the pain he is feeling right now.

"You can't lose hope, you can't know for sure," I say hopefully.

He looks up at me and gently caresses a hand to my cheek. "I wish I could be as positive as you," he says softly. He collects himself and rises to his feet again. "If he is projecting an illusion that he is my father, then that means he is our hidden light magic we are looking for. Now we just need to find out who he is," Aiden says composing himself. "Who-ever that man is posing as my father should be back today, so until we figure out what's going on, we have to play things safe, okay?" He walks over to me, wrapping his arms around my waist.

"Whatever I say, you have to promise not to take anything seriously but still give me back as you always have done. We can't let anyone know things have changed between us, okay?" Aiden demands.

"Okay," I reply, a little relieved.

He leans his head down to kiss me, his lips softly caress mine.

We are just finishing the last of our meal when the king arrives. Aiden rises to greet him as he usually does, his control impresses me.

"How was your trip, father?" Aiden asks.

"Quite well, thank you for asking. My brother has everything perfectly in hand in the east now, so there is nothing to worry about," he says, beaming back at the both of us.

"Enough about my trip. How are you two love birds doing?" he says happily.

Aiden and I look at each other and Aiden snaps his head, looking away from me. I quickly copy him, sneering as I do.

The king chuckles. "Oh well, these things take time," he says, beaming at us both.

"I doubt that," Aiden huffs. We finish our meal and Aiden rises from the table. "We will take our leave now. Welcome home, father," Aiden bows his head to his father and stands behind my chair, pulling it out so I can rise.

"Welcome home, Your Majesty," I say with a smile.

He reaches out for my hand and kisses it. The whiskers from his beard brush against my hand. "Thank you and good night," he retorts.

I smile a little wider. "Good night, Your Majesty," I respond.

We walk back to our room in our usual silence. Aiden removes his belt, sword, and jacket as usual, laying them out on the chair at the door, but when he sits on the bed to remove his boots, he pauses, looking at the floor.

"What's wrong?" I ask.

It takes him a moment to reply. "Your right, that man is not my father," Aiden mutters darkly.

"You saw the real him and not the illusion? How did you know to call him father?" I comment.

"When I saw who he really was, all my worst fears came to light," he exclaims.

"Who is he?" I ask, more worried than ever.

"He is your father, Bree," Aiden announces.

13

Midoria

"The very man I have been trying to protect you from is here pulling all the strings," Aiden says through gritted teeth as he paces the floor, throwing his hands in his hair.

My heart is pounding in my chest at his words. "What do you mean?" I ask.

Aiden looks at me, noticing he has said something he was not meant to. He sighs. "When you were twelve, the night I took you to the crystal cave," he starts...

"You mean the night where you pushed me into the portal?" I ask sharply.

"Yes," Aiden replies cautiously, raising an eyebrow. "I did that because I snuck into the castle to see you, as I always did, and overheard your father talking about taking your life to feed a power source that would destroy all magic, leaving light magic to rule over the remnants of the land, and now you're right back where he wants you," he admits to me.

That's why my father did all this, to keep me close. He thought fake bonding me with Aiden, and knowing how much he hates light magic, he figured I would be safer as his bonded. This would also stop me from being tossed out, or killed on sight, or even taken by another man that would have me. But he didn't know Aiden and I knew each other as children.

"What do we do now?" I ask. Aiden, still lost in his own thoughts, doesn't seem to hear me. "Aiden," I say again. He finally looks at me.

"Father...I mean your father has said all his trips have been to sort kingdom affairs with my uncle, I think we should start there," he says.

"Okay, so to your uncle it is. How do we explain our leaving?" I ask.

"I don't know," Aiden admits.

I don't know what to say. This new information has my head spinning. Aiden notices my desperate need for answers about my father, and that night.

"I'm sorry, I don't know much more. I was only a boy myself, but all I know is it scared me, and I wanted nothing more than to protect you," he says caressing my hand as he sits beside me. "I promise I'll protect you. Together we will find the answers and stop it from ever happening. All I know is, things can't be good if he's here in my father's place just when you come back," he adds, trying to comfort me.

The following morning, Aiden takes me out to the Lillulian orchard. My excitement is bursting out of me. Lillulian's are the fruits Madeline packs in my lunches that I take every day to the bloom tree. Madeline knows it's my favorite. The fruit is a small, yellow and orange grape size fruit that opens like a banana and tastes like a cherry mango.

The carriage ride is breathtaking with all the Lillulian trees lining the road. They're big, and the fruit drapes from the trees like grapes hanging from a vine. They have beautiful flowers that remind me of a very colorful passionflower. When we get further down my excitement is taken from me rather abruptly. When we arrive, there is a mass of people waiting for us. They race over to Aiden. They are all trying to talk to him at once.

"ENOUGH!" Aiden bellows, they all quiet down and take a step back from us. "Okay, now one at a time. What is all the fuss about?" he asks calmly.

"It's the Lillulian trees!" one worker replies.

"Yeah, there is something wrong with them," another continues.

"Come see!"

We are pushed deeper into the orchard, and it is not hard to see what all the fuss is about. The further we go the worse it gets; the trees seem to be infected.

"Um, Aiden don't they look like those crystals on the Akuma?" I enquire.

"Yes," Aiden says, with a scowl on his face as he looks over the tree. "It looks exactly like the crystals on the Akuma because they are capium crystals."

The entire entourage of workers gasp and step back from the trees.

"How is this possible? I thought there was only one place that had these and it was a dangerous place to go?" I ask.

"That's because it is and this is not supposed to be here. Something is very wrong." Aiden throws his hands in his hair as he thinks.

The frightened chatter goes on around us. I think for a moment.

"Ah Aiden," I murmur.

"Yes, what is it?" he enquires.

"It might not be anything helpful, but I think I remember seeing capium in a few potion recipes I saw in my book," I say.

Aiden looks at me. "What do you mean? How does that help? Anything that uses capium can't be good, it's used in dark magic," Aiden expresses angrily.

"I know you said that, but what I mean is, I saw something about curing someone that had been poisoned by it. If I make up the cure in my book, do you think it could cure the orchard?" I ask.

The voices around us start up again, but now voices are directing their questions to me.

"Oh my, can she do that?" someone whispers.

"I don't know, can you do that?" someone else enquires.

"Can you save the orchard?" they ask me.

Aiden looks at me with the same question on his face.

"I don't know, but if you let me, I would love to try," I respond.

"Okay, let's give it a try," Aiden announces.

I race back to the carriage and grab my bag, digging through it for my book. I open it to the page I'm looking for.

"Ah, here it is," I say as the group slowly catches up to me. I show Aiden the potion.

"This looks promising," he says.

"But this might be a big problem, look, here all the ingredients are easy enough to acquire except this," he says pointing to the book.

I look where he is pointing. "What is Prillum?" I ask.

"It's a flowering vine that grows only in one place," Aiden says with a grim expression.

"Let me guess, the capium fields?" I groan.

"Yes," Aiden says.

"Okay, so what we need to do is organize a team to go to the fields, find the flowers, and bring them back. We can get everyone else to get the rest of the ingredients together for when we return," I confirm.

"Good. That was exactly what I was thinking," Aiden says. "But you and I are going to lead the team."

"Wait, what?" I exclaim.

"We wanted a reason to leave and investigate your father, I think we just got it. We have to go through Midoria, where my uncle is, to get there. It's perfect."

I sigh. "I was hoping my first trip out would not be a dangerous one," I complain.

Aiden raises an eyebrow at me. "So, you're saying you would happily send others out to do something you wouldn't do yourself?" he remarks.

"Uh, no! I didn't mean that!" I stammer.

"Remember, I said those of us with magic need to protect those without. It's our duty."

I look at the ground a little ashamed of myself.

"On another note, do I want to ask where you got this book?"

"Your... I... ah... mean my father gave it to me shortly after I got here," I admit.

Aiden turns from me, giving directions to the workers to close off the affected trees as best as they can. I look through my book again for something I remember seeing before.

"Aiden!" I call to him.

Aiden returns to my side, a little annoyed.

"Can you get me a lot of the local rocks from around the orchard?" I ask.

"Sure, why?" he asks, confused.

"We have no idea how it's traveled so far, so I thought we might have more time if I use a barrier spell and all I need is local rocks from around the infected area to create it. What do you think?" I ask hopefully.

"Do you really believe we can trust that book?" he asks.

"I really do," I answer honestly.

"Then I think you are brilliant, and it might be our best chance," he says.

I transfer a little light magic onto each rock surrounding the infected space. When the last stone is placed, a large barrier shoots up surrounding the entire area. The shouts and cheers boom through the air. I smile at the happy cheers directed at me. The feeling makes my heart swell with delight. I even catch a little look of pride on Aiden's face for a brief moment that makes me even happier.

We return to the castle and get the preparations underway for our long trip to Midoria. With no time to lose, we give directions for the ingredients to be collected and all the arrangements to keep things going while we are gone.

We don't see my father and I'm glad of it, too. I have not seen him since Aiden told me King Darnell was not who I thought he was all this time, but my own father instead. If I was to see him now, I don't know how to talk to him. We leave him word we are on a mission to save the orchard and leave that night.

The ride takes a few days to get there, but sometime in the afternoon, Aiden wakes me from my sleep.

"Bree," he says, gently stroking my hair.

I stir. "Mmmhm." My eyes flutter open to Aiden's beautiful blue eyes. "Mmmmm hello." I say groggily.

"We are here," Aiden says.

I shoot up to see. My mouth falls open as I look out the carriage window to a city made of green.

"It's so green," I say.

Aiden laughs slightly. "Yes, it is, this is Midoria. It's the elemental city of earth-focused magic."

I look at Aiden with a snap of my neck. "Are you saying there are other elemental towns?" I ask in excitement.

"Yes!" Aiden replies with a smile, delighted at my excitement. "There are four main elemental cities. Midoria: earth magic, Exidore: the fire city, Sky town: wind, and Aquilla: the city of water," he explains.

"Oh, wow!" I exclaim. "I can't wait to explore this place!"

Aiden frowns at me.

"I know you're excited, but you have to remember we are on a very important mission. We are looking for information about what your father is up to, why he's visiting here all the time, and gathering a team to get us through to the capium fields without dying," he states pointedly.

I sigh, knowing his right.

We cross over a large, wooden vine bridge and see a load of couples in little round boats on the river below, Aiden leans over me to see what I'm looking at and smiles.

"Those are coracles. Traditionally they would be made of animal skin and tar, but here they're made of sticks moss, and oil," he explains.

"Couples come from far and wide during the infinity festival to build them with their partners. It's a show that their boats are as strong as their bonds. I'll take you some time if you like," he says.

I beam at him. "Yes, I would like that very much!" I say with more excitement than I thought possible.

The carriage pulls up outside the front of a big castle, not as grand as the one back home, but it's charming. The entire castle is made of thousands of trees molding together to make an exquisite castle. The steps are wood with wooden railings wrapped in vines that lead the way up to the massive, wooden double doors.

When we reach the top, we are greeted by a butler with dark brown leaves that line the back of his head. His flesh is a light green with light brown eyes. His clothes are a suit of moss and bark. We follow him, and he leads us through the grand entrance. I try very hard to keep my mouth closed as we walk into the castle. This is unbelievable! Never in my wildest dreams could I ever think something like this could exist. As we walk, the floor goes from wood to grass, carpeted with tiny red flowers.

We are led to an office in one of the side rooms. When we enter, a man pulls his head up from a stack of paperwork on his desk. From everything I've seen so far, I don't know why I was expecting him to be green, but he is not. He's very handsome and looks a lot like his brother, King Darnell, with black hair the same as Aiden, except dusted with grey showing a little of his age, but unlike Aiden, his eyes are grey.

"Uncle, it's so good to see you," Aiden says, holding out a greeting hand to him.

"Good to see you, too," he replies, taking Aiden's hand in his.

"And who is this dazzling beauty?" he asks, taking my hand and pressing a gentle kiss to it.

Aiden lets a low growl rumble through his throat in warning. "Uncle." he warns.

A giggle escapes from me as I answer. "Hello, my name is Bree," I declare.

"She is my bonded Uncle, so don't get any ideas," Aiden huffs.
I smile at his jealousy.

"I'm Jonathan, this charming young man's uncle," he beams.

"Thank you for such a lovely greeting. It's been so long since I have been treated with such hospitality, as you can imagine. I didn't think..."

He cuts me off. "You thought you would be treated unkindly?" he asks.

"Well, yes," I admit.

"Because of you being of light magic?" he asks.

"Yes," I say, in almost a whisper.

"Though people are afraid, you have many more that have spoken of the incredible things you have done. Believe it or not, you have a lot of supporters saying you're not like others we have known, and word of what you did for the Lillulian orchards has spread very fast throughout the kingdoms. Don't be surprised more won't greet you the same," he states.

This new information has my heart aflutter with hope.

"On a different note. How is everything back home? And how is my dear brother?" Jonathan asks.

"Actually Uncle, that is exactly why we are here," Aiden replies.

"Nothing's wrong is it? I thought I would have heard something if it was," he retorts worriedly.

"No, no. We just wanted to know what business you and father had, to keep him coming here so much lately," Aiden asks.

Jonathan screws his face up in confusion. "I... ah... don't know what you're talking about. I have not seen my brother since a few months before Bree arrived here," he answers.

Aiden and I look at each other.

"What is going on?" Jonathan asks.

"We are here for some good men to take us through the capium fields," Aiden says, trying to change the subject.

Jonathan raises an eyebrow at Aiden. "I'll get you a team. It won't be easy for what you are asking, but it's doable. On the other note, what is going on?" he asks, folding his arms, not budging from the subject.

We spend the rest of the night telling Jonathan all that has happened until now. Aiden obviously trusts his uncle very much. Apparently, Jonathan knew all about our time together as kids, too, so he didn't have much to catch up on.

"What in the name of magic did that bastard do to my brother?" he yells angrily. He paces, throwing his hands in his hair. *It must be a family trait*, I think, smiling inside at the thought.

"We don't know, that's what we are here to find out. He said all the trips he was going on were to see his brother to deal with the affairs of the kingdom," Aiden replies.

I gasp and place my hand on Aiden's arm to stop him. "Do you think he meant my uncle?" I ask.

"You don't have an uncle."

"Remember the strange man I told you about that killed my mother?"

"Yes, of course."

"Well, I remember him telling me to call him Uncle after that."

"He made you call him Uncle after he killed your mother in front of you? That is messed up," Aiden says, disgust soaking his words. "Honestly, it would make a hell of a lot of sense that if your father is alive, there have to be more hiding in plain sight."

"This sounds really dangerous, you two need to play this safe. Now, I know I'll play along for now if he comes my way, but just be careful. Anything you need, I'll be happy to help," Jonathan says. "I'll get a team together by first light. You two get some sleep, you're going to need it."

14

Not What It Seems

Just as he said bright and early, but it's Jonathan's wife that greets us. Oh my, this makes so much sense now. She is the breathtaking green elemental beauty I saw at the ball four nights ago.

"Hello again, I'm Aria," she greets me, offering me her hand. I take it tentatively.

"Um, yes, it's nice to see you again," I stammer.

"Oh, don't worry, dear child. If you're worried about me, you need not trouble yourself. I saw what happened and I made sure to quash any horrid rumor that tried its way through here. It was horrid how they spoke to you. If that adorable little protector didn't stand up for you, I would have," she says pointedly. I smile.

"Thank you, that cute little protector of mine was my deerling," I say, as it appears rolling on the grass, having a good old scratch at her feet.

She giggles in delight. "How darling," Aria says, squatting down to touch it.

My deerling hops into her hand as it accepts her pets happily. Absentmindedly, Aria leads us out the doors, not looking up from the deerling.

"Good morning, my dearest," Jonathan says, greeting his wife with a kiss to her temple.

"Good morning," she replies lovingly.

Wrapping an arm around Aria's waist, Jonathan waves a hand to a group of twenty people.

"Here is a great team I have pulled together for you. They should be able to handle anything you may come across. Okay, lady and gents, introduce yourselves, please," Jonathan says authoritatively.

"Hey there, I'm Metikye, nice to meet chya, I'm from Exidor, ya find ya self in strife, I can burn the place down and get chya out," he says, proudly, in a deep voice. His long black hair falls down his back, but at that moment a light breeze blows, ruffling his hair slightly, enough to see fire red, shift through his hair as it moves.

"I hope it doesn't come to that, but it's great to have you on board," Aiden replies.

"Nathaniel here, I'm your tracker," a tall man with short well-kept ash-blond hair says.

"MacNeil," a man a bit older than the rest, with short dark brown hair and a tidy beard and mustache says in a loud voice. "But you can call me Mac, I'll have your bodyguard detail with Luc over there." He nods over to a stocky man with shoulder-length blond hair.

"Hi I'm Luc, I hate my name but Luc is better than my full name. he winces I'll have your back day or night."

A tall, beautiful woman with very long, golden-brown dreadlocks in a high ponytail steps forward, her brown skin setting off her deep blue eyes. "I'm Roxy, I'm your weapons specialist. Just because I'm a woman, don't think I can't hold my own because you will be seriously mistaken," she says with a confident smile.

"This is Logan." A man with snow-white shoulder-length hair steps forward. "He is from Sky Town. He doesn't say much, but he will give you air support and keep the winds in your favor. These six will lead the other fourteen members of your party. You will have everything you will need," Jonathan says proudly crossing his arms. "You are traveling northeast towards the dangerous lands, due to the terrain, a carriage would never get through, so I've obtained Andocrits to transport you and the supplies you will need to cross the dangerous lands," Jonathan adds.

I approach the Andocrits. Its large with thick dreadlocked fur. A saddle is strapped to its back, with large sacks bigger than me, strapped to each side of it. I hold my hand out as I approach, giving it a chance to get used to me first. With no reaction, I approach carefully, and run my hand along its leathery head that is four times bigger than my own. I run my fingers through its dreaded mane that runs down its neck to blend in with the rest of its body.

It stretches one of its tattered bat-like wings out to me, and I assume it's providing a way up onto its back. The moment I'm seated, the Andocrit moves, and the ground shoots away from me quickly. The large mass of dreaded fur was hiding four very long thin legs under it. I'm just getting my racing heart under control, when Aiden and the others join us.

"Are you ready to move?" he asks.

I look to the ground that I'm so far away from now. "I guess so," I stammer.

He smiles at me. "This is the best and most comfortable way to get there," he replies.

Metikye leads the way with Logan. Not wanting to argue any further with Aiden, I'm stuck in the middle with the other men, while Roxy, Aiden, and Nathaniel bring up the rear, as Luc and Mac circle the perimeter of the group. The terrain begins to get rocky as we leave the path and start to climb. I'm unable to enjoy the new flora and fauna as I'm just trying to get used to the motion of the andocrit.

The only way I can think of explaining it, is how it would feel in a boat on rough seas, with large waves pushing the boat up and down as they pass underneath it. Aiden notices and hands me a small leather sac.

"You can use this if you..."

Aiden doesn't finish the sentence before I'm ejecting the contents of my stomach into the bag. After a while, I pull my head up, feeling safe to do so. Aiden hands me a flask of water and a root of some kind.

"Chew on this, it will ease your stomach. We still have a long way to go," he assures me.

"What is it?" I ask as I tear a piece of it with my teeth. It's like I'm chewing a jerky carrot. I'm instantly feeling much better.

"I think it's better if you don't know what it is."

My stomach drops at the thought of what it could be, but since it is helping and I don't want to test the limits of my stomach, I don't push the issue any further. With my stomach feeling much better, I notice my surroundings much more. We are not climbing anymore; we are traveling through a high-top valley.

The trees look sick, and the grass is brown. The further we go, the worse the land gets, until it looks like a fire has blown through ravaging the area. Black trees, like charcoal, and bright orange crystals dot the rocks, and protrude from the trees with a light frosting over the grass and leaves. We come to a large clearing before nightfall, and set up camp for the night. All the andocrits circle our camp.

Metikye goes to the center of the space and ignites a large flame that snakes around his body, then shoots up in the air, exploding like a firework above us. As it falls, the fire creates a burning dome around our camp.

"Wow!" I say, the words leaving my lips before I can think.

Metikye strolls over to us with a grin on his face at my reaction.

"If a small trick like that can impress you, I doubt you could handle me in action," he says with a wink.

I blush. "I'm sorry, I'm still learning and where I was raised you don't see anything like that," I admit.

"It's quite alright, I know I'm amazen." Metikye says puffing out his chest.

I giggle as he gives me a funny smile, making me more relaxed.

The men that we brought with us busy themselves setting up

blankets to sleep on and preparing food. After dinner almost everyone goes to bed.

Aiden is doing rounds with Metikye, and Logan and Roxy are getting a little sleep before they change over. At some point, Logan has given up trying to sleep, like me. I offer a very tired Aiden and Metikye an early change over, which Logan seems happy to offer, too. Aiden gives me a curious look that asks if I'm sure I'll be okay.

"I'll be with Logan, I'll be fine. Go get some sleep, I promise I'll wake you if I get tired," I say, interrupting his thoughts.

Some time goes by until the silence becomes deafening.

"I wish I knew why you don't talk. I could not imagine anyone hurting you, not to mention if you have powers. Aren't you supposed to be royalty somehow? And if you are, how did you come to be with Jonathan?" I look over to a wide-eyed, very overwhelmed Logan. "I'm so sorry, Logan. I have so many questions. I can't help myself. Not to mention, it's been so long since I had a friend to talk to. Everyone back home is afraid of me, except for Madeline that is, but it's not very pleasant at all. I find myself hiding away, not wanting to talk to anyone either," I say a tad too fast.

"Why?" Logan asks.

"Why what?" I ask in return. Then my eyes shoot open as I realize Logan just talked to me.

"Why are they afraid?"

Trying not to make a big fuss out of him conversating, I simply answer. "Honestly, I don't understand myself, because of my light magic people seem to be afraid of me, because of things others have done before me. I'm me, not them. I wish they would just give me a chance," I say a little sad.

"Light magic, huh?" Logan says.

I nod slightly.

"Well, I don't care. You seem okay to me."

I smile at Logan who gives me a little smile back. "Are you going to tell me a bit about yourself?" I ask.

Logan chuckles. For the next few hours, we talk and talk. I feel like Logan needed someone to talk to just as much as I did.

"Metikye and I have powers, that is true, but we have found the family we have made is far greater than the ones we were given that abandoned us. We support each other and care about all the members of our family."

I yawn as Logan looks over my head with a smile. I turn to see Aiden coming for change over.

"I think that's it for one night," he smiles. "Welcome to the family, Bree," Logan says, turning and going back to camp.

I smile brightly, my heart at bursting point.

"What has you so happy?" Aiden says, a little annoyed.

I bump my shoulder into his with a smile. "Don't be jealous." I whisper.

"Who said I was jealous?" He growls.

I giggle, wrapping my arms around him. "I'm happy because it looks like I made a new friend," I beam.

Aiden smiles into my hair, squeezing me tighter. "I think you have made a lot of new friends, Bree," Aiden says, pressing a kiss to the top of my head. "Just don't get too friendly with any of them," he says warningly.

I give him a light push and giggle at his possessiveness.

"You better get off to sleep, you need your rest," Aiden replies, gently rubbing my back.

I give him a kiss and do just that.

Sometime through the night a crack of thunder roars above us. The sky opens up but no rain falls. I fall back to sleep listening to the soothing sound. Light begins to drift through, lighting the sky. The rain still sounds over us. I open my eyes to see the Andocrits have extended their wings out above us, protecting our camp from the rain.

I walk over to my Andocrit with a towel in hand. She nestles her face into me lazily as I rub the towel over her, drying her as best as I can. "All night you all protected us from the rain, thank you for that," I say, planting a light kiss to her cheek. The rain is light now, but the sky remains cloudy.

Everyone is bustling about now preparing food, tending to their travel companions, and packing up camp. I look around and notice the fire is gone.

"Oh, Metikye, it seems rain is not your friend," I say cheekily.

Metikye meets my challenging tone. "Fire and water never get along, but you can't have one without the other, life is too complex to allow it, and I wasn't too fussed, as it's not likely anything would challenge the storm to get to us out here anyway," he replies casually.

Nathaniel, Roxy, and Logan appear from the trees up ahead. Aiden meets up with them and I go to see what's going on.

"There are some big tracks up ahead. They have been washed out from the rain, but you can still see that a group of Akuma has traveled through here within the last day or so. We need to stay on high alert as they could be close by waiting out the storm before we got here," Nathaniel says.

"I'll make sure everyone is armed appropriately to handle them if it comes to that," Roxy answers.

"The plant you seek grows a few hours further northeast, but due to the storm we should have very little disturbances from the local wildlife, and our scent should be dulled as well by the rain," Nathaniel continues.

A few hours have passed, and the woods around us are sparse, black, and very un-inviting. The smell of mold in the air is thick, making it hard to take a good breath.

Metikye, Logan, and Roxy have stopped. Aiden and I move to their side. We are looking out over a large, wide-based tree ahead laden with prillum. Around its mass is a wall of capium. A thud sounds behind us, startling all of us to look behind us. One of our men has fallen from his andocrit and is writhing on the ground. I gasp. The other men are not looking too good either.

"What is going on?" I ask.

Metikye moves behind us, moving his men quickly. "Move back now," he commands. His men obey him immediately.

Quickly, and not wanting to go any further, Logan and Roxy get off their travel companions to attend to the man on the ground, while Metikye ushers the rest back a safe distance away.

"What's going on? The prillum is just up ahead. We are almost there," I say, confused.

"The capium in this area is too strong, it's making everyone sick. We need to go back and find another way!" Metikye commands authoritatively.

I look back at the tree and push my andocrit ahead. Startled, Aiden chases after me.

"What do you think you're doing? You can't go off on your own!" he shouts at me.

"You said it yourself, we have a duty to fulfill and we are almost there," I reply, my determination evident.

We get to the tree and Aiden and I get to work gathering the prillum, quickly pulling the vines from the tree, and carefully removing the flowers from the vine. The flowers are made up of large petals made of what looks like fine lace. Aiden gives a big tug on a vine and falls backward, bumping into a big wall of capium. A yelp falls from his mouth, and a large burn like mark appears on his arm.

"I think we have more than enough," I say, pushing Aiden back to his andocrit. I stuff the last of the prillum into his storage bag on the back of his andocrit. "Let's go," I order.

Roxy, Logan, and Metikye are waiting for us a little way up the trail.

"Oh, thank the elements!" Roxy and Metikye say at the same time, sweat beaded across their brows.

"That was so stupid going off like that! We look back to find ya both ran off! How is this not affectin' either of ya?" Metikye asks.

"I honestly don't know, but I think my tolerance comes from Bree somehow," Aiden admits, a little perplexed too.

"I thought chya were dead for sure. I'm glad ya not but I thought it," Metikye babbles.

"I don't know but we got what we came for. Let's check on the men and get as far away from here as we can," I say quickly.

"Agreed," Roxy replies.

A loud howl carries through the air. Our pace picks up quickly, when screams and roars sound up ahead. As we get closer, Metikye's men are running, and fighting a large pack of Akuma that are descending on them.

Hurriedly, we pass two Akuma playing tug of war with an Andocrit, tearing it apart, as another kicks and flails its wings, fighting off three Akuma. Howls and cries sound off all around us. Metikye's flames fly through the sky, fighting off the mass attack.

I look over to find Aiden has abandoned his Andocrit and is holding off a large group that seems to be fighting his magic persuasion. One breaks through, launching toward him.

"Aiden!" I scream.

Logan catches it in mid-air, at the same time a second one comes at Aiden from behind. He knocks it backwards into a group of them coming to join the fight. Logan throws the Akuma he is holding in the air, into a nearby bush.

I sigh in relief. Aiden looks at me, giving me an, 'I'm okay' look, then seeing I'm safe, retreats to help the others. Before I can even catch my breath, an Akuma team attacks my andocrit, clamping onto her throat and front legs, tearing her down to the ground. I manage to jump off her at the last moment before she hits the ground with a horrible thud.

Once she is down, they turn to stalk toward me slowly. My andocrit is unable to move. I see her struggling to get to me. Whimpers and cries fall from her as she struggles with everything in her to get up, but fails. The sound brings tears to my eyes.

I look over and to see Aiden, Roxy, Logan, Luc, Mac and a few of the others are being pressed in on, just like me. I can't let anyone else get hurt. I have to do something. An Akuma dives at Aiden and I lose it, panic courses through me.

"AIDEN!" I scream.

A pulse wave shoots from my body, throwing everything away from me. Yelps and cries ring out as I run to Aiden, my deerling flashing to life, blazing a bright blinding light in front of him and his group.

Our team members cover their faces and fall to their knees. The Akuma whimper and yelp, turning on their heels and scattering as far and as fast as they can.

Metikye bursts from overhead, chasing after them on his andocrit, a lasso of fire circling above him. He throws it down at their heels, pushing them further from the remnants of the group.

I race to Aiden's side, making sure he's okay, as my deerling protectively strides the area, checking on everyone and leading a member of the team to someone needing help.

Aiden throws his arms around me when I reach him, kissing me hard. I kiss him back equally as hard, desperate for the contact. I throw my hands in his hair, pulling him to me harder as he fists his hands on mine, deepening the kiss. I don't know how long we kissed, but the gratitude the other was okay rang through the moment clearly.

"Ahem." A throat clears close by. It's Roxy. "I'm sorry to interrupt the moment."

Aiden and I pull away realizing the situation still at hand.

We attend to the wounded men and andocrit's doing what we can. I'm glad I made up a big batch of different levels of healing balms from my book for the trip. They have come in handy and are working very well from slight abrasions to large gashes. Besides Roxy, Logan, Nathaniel, Luc, Mac, Aiden, Metikye and I, only four others survived the attack. I'm closing off a chunk of missing flesh from one man's right side, while Aiden and Roxy hold down another one of the men as Logan and Metikye put pressure to the bloody stump where his right leg used to be.

After the wounded men are patched up and settled, we move on to helping the andocrit's. The healing medicines work just as well on them, too, and we manage to get ten healed up and back on their feet.

I'm finishing up with the last one when my deerling tugs at me.

I follow him to where my andocrit lies. I gasp, falling to her side. Her throat has massive gashes, and her breathing has almost stopped. Frantically, I rub a load of the remaining medicines on her in hopes it will do something, but I know it won't be enough. I throw my arms around her head and bury my face into her cheek as my tears fall in a violent flood.

"I'm so sorry I couldn't protect you. I am so sorry!" I wail.

She stretches her wing over me, holding me to her. I feel her breath one last time. Looking up, I see the life leave her eyes, her tattered wing going slack, her loving embrace gone.

I don't know how long I have been crying but it's Aiden's arm that brings me back. Wrapping his arm around my waist, he pulls me to him, and I feel my tears slow a little. Just being close to him helps ease the pain.

"We have salvaged what we can and packed them up on the remaining andocrit's, but there are not enough for all of us. We can ride together on one of the lighter packed andocrit's," he says.

I nod and slowly make my way to my feet with Aiden's help. I take one last look at my travel companion and watch as Logan gently lifts her body in the air with his magic, lowering her into a grave that has been dug for her. The wind spirals around the large dirt mound next to the grave, and covers her body with a gracefulness so honoring to her, leaving a single Perillum flower atop her resting place.

After all those we lost have been buried and the remainder of us packed and ready to go, Aiden holds out a hand to me to help me up behind him. When I hear a sound behind me, I turn to see my deerling toddle off behind a large bush. I creep forward slowly.

"What is it?" Aiden asks, climbing down to follow me.

I move behind the bush and freeze. My deerling is standing next to a wounded Akuma. The wounded Akuma seems unafraid of me. Slowly, I move closer to it and notice this Akuma is not going anywhere. It looks like all four of its legs are broken in more places than I can count, I think shattered might be a better word for her legs.

I shriek and jump back in terror as another Akuma leaps out at me. Its claws come flying in my direction. In a flash the Akuma is intercepted in mid-air by the wounded one that was on the ground.

Latching onto its jugular, it sinks its teeth in deeper until the Akuma in its mouth stops fighting. After a few moments I assume it's dead as its lifeless body is released from the wounded Akuma's mouth.

It just looks at me. I step closer, and all of a sudden it yelps and whimpers, desperately trying to get to its feet but its legs have nothing left. Aiden pushes in front of me spear raised above his head.

"NO!" I yell as its eyes widen in fear, I throw myself in front of it, stopping him in his tracks.

"What do you think you're doing?" he snarls. "That thing does not deserve your kindness," he spits.

"This Akuma just saved my life," I reply defensively.

I look back at it. My deerling is still at its side. Slowly, I step closer to it. Something is pulling me, a feeling I think Aiden feels as well because I see him lower the weapon to his side.

The creature seems to see we are not threatening her and quietens down. I approach her very cautiously. She must be the Akuma Logan threw from Aiden when I screamed because all four of her legs look broken from a fall like that.

She rests her head on the ground in front of her as I move to her back legs, examining them. I think she is trying to make me more comfortable and willing to help her if her mouth is facing away from me, which I am grateful for.

I lean into the bush where I see some sticks I can use as splints. I rip at the hem of my jacket for some material to secure them to her leg. She howls an ear-piercing howl as I set the right leg and tie it in place.

"THAT HURT!" screams through my head. My eyes grow wide as I look to Aiden who looks the same.

"You heard it, too?" I explode at him, unbelieving.

"Yes," he replies, equally shocked.

"My magic gives me the ability to talk and understand all creatures, but I was trying to communicate with the Akuma but couldn't. I thought the capium was the reason. I think our bond is getting stronger, if you can share this ability and maybe even amplify it to reach the Akuma," Aiden comments.

"Great, you can understand me, woohoo." says the voice dryly. "That really hurt! Think you could be gentler?" it asks.

"How about you be more grateful we didn't kill you," Aiden snaps back.

She huffs, placing her head back on the ground in front of her. My deerling comes back awkwardly, dragging some sticks to my side. I giggle as I take them. Aiden gets some rags I can use to bandage her up, and I reset each leg as gently and as quickly as I can. After the Akuma is all patched up, she turns her head to me.

"Thank you," she breathes.

"It's my honor," I reply. "I don't know what to do now. If we leave you here, you will surely die. We will have to take you with us until you're healed," I say.

"You would do that for me?" she asks, surprised.

"Of course, it's the least I can do. After all, you did save my life and I'm sure if you wanted me dead you would not have intervened," I state.

"I never had any intention to hurt you or your friends. I sensed his magic and tried to talk to him, but before I could, I saw the Akuma try to attack him from behind. I tried to help but I was sent flying before I could even get close," she says, nodding in Aiden's direction.

Aiden opens his mouth to say something but then decides against it, closing his mouth again.

"I tried to warn you before they attacked, too," she adds.

"The howl we first heard, that was you?" I ask.

"Yes" she replies.

15

❦

Betrayal

"Thank you, if not for the warning, I doubt there would be as many of us left as there is," I say.

She lowers her head onto her two front paws. "Not as many as I'd hoped," she sighs.

"Aren't you upset about your pack?" I ask.

"That was not my pack. I don't have one, I've been following you since you came up into the valley," she replies.

"You could have attacked us at any time," I say, a little shocked.

"Yes, I guess I could have, if that was my intention, but you do have some good men. That should bring you some comfort," she replies.

"If we are to be together, I would prefer it if you had a name," I say.

She thinks for a moment. "Rei, call me Rei." she answers.

"That's a beautiful name," I comment.

Aiden looks at Rei and I, still standing by like a bodyguard, I'm sure to intervene if Rei decided to hurt me, but I'm sure Aiden feels it too, that Rei wouldn't hurt us.

"Okay, Rei, we are going to have to get you on one of our andocrits to transport you. It will be a big journey, but I promise to stay with you the whole time and manage your pain along the way."

Aiden's crossed arms fly to his sides, clenching into fists. "You are traveling with me," he says, through clenched teeth.

"I can't just leave her to someone else, they won't even understand why Rei is with us, let alone why we are helping an Akuma. Come on, Aiden, you know it's the only way this will work."

Aiden looks at Rei with a fierce look, then turns and storms off. I look back to Rei after I can no longer see Aiden.
"I'm sorry."

"It's quite all right, child, I understand. Please don't be upset. He just wants you safe that's all. I can see how much he loves you," a smile dances across my lips.

"I know he does, and no less than I love him, but he needs to trust me as I trust him," I sigh.

"Oh, but trusting you in a situation that puts his desire to protect you at risk is a very hard thing to ask of any man. A war is waging in him right now. Please don't push him. I can travel beside you. We can stop if we must, but I do think it's best if you put him at ease first," Rei replies.

"No, Bree travels with you."

We both snap our heads in his direction, where Aiden is standing, Logan at his side.

"I appreciate your words, but I do trust Bree above all. It's you I don't trust. I know Bree is right, no one would be calm with you or know the healing she does, nor do they understand you, and the andocrit will not carry you without her, but mark my words, you breathe on her in a way I don't like I'll have you calved up and on the next fire that I see," Aiden warns.

I know he's right, they're all the reasons I said what I did. My heart swells that he trusts me even though it hurts him that my safety is at risk.

Logan doesn't ask questions, not that he says anything around others in the first place. He simply pushes the wind under Rei and lifts her onto the andocrits back where a box-like saddle sits.

"Roxy made it up. It will be more comfortable for it to travel," Aiden informs me.

"Her name is Rei," I say, annoyed.

"IT is lucky, IT is not dead," he retorts.

I sigh as I climb up to sit behind Rei.

"No matter, child," Rei says, moving to curl herself around me.

"What are you doing?" I ask.

"You will be far more comfortable resting against me. This was modified for me, not you. Not to mention, you are at a far greater risk of being hurt by my spikes behind me than at my chest, and my body should keep you warm, too," Rei answers.

"Aiden won't like this." I look over to where he's watching us unapprovingly.

"Hush. I'll deal with his wrath if I must, but you know I speak the truth."

Looking behind her, I see all the capium crystal spikes at her heels and back. That would have me on guard the whole trip back. A little relieved, I sink down against her side.

"Wow, you are extremely comfortable. With all the hard scales and crystal spikes you wouldn't guess," I say in wonder.

A little laugh leaves her. "Yes, I guess that would be easy to assume, but the spot you are in is a very unguarded spot, making it the safest spot for you," Rei says.

"Rei, did you just tell me your weakness?" I ask, accusatory.

"Yes, I guess I did," she chuckles.

"Why would you do that?" I ask.

"You trust me right now and I'm positive you will protect my secret." She brings her head around, so her body is almost a circle around me now. "I'm sorry, child. I don't have the energy to talk any more. I'll protect you and keep you warm as best I can, but my energy is depleted. I must rest now," Rei says, sleepily drifting off.

Over the next couple of days, Rei has slept most of the way. She is healing much quicker than I thought possible. I wake her now and then feed her and give her water, but most of the time she just sleeps. Aiden travels at my side. He seems more relaxed now than before and far less tense.

Rei's warmth and size have protected me from most of the wind and cold. Aiden even threw a blanket to me to cover over Rei, and Metikye made a fire lasso around us all at the worst of it, to keep us all warm, but no one expected him to keep it up as long as he did. Now Aiden has taken the lead so Metikye can recoup his strength.

"How are you feeling?" I ask Metikye, now at my side.

He looks weak but a brief moment of strength pushes onto his face. "Me? Oh, I'm fantastic. Couldn't be betta don't chya worry about me, little miss," he flashes me his best smile.

I flash one back. "Liar," I grin.

He looks at me with a pout, letting his facade slip a little. "I'll be alright, don't chya worry bout me," Metikye replies.

"I do, and I will, and lying to me will only make me worry more," I say with a pout.

He smiles a genuine smile. "I know, I'm sorry. I am feelin betta I swear. I'll be back good as new before ya know it, alright?"

I sigh. "Okay, but I'm watching you," I say warningly.

He smiles and lets his eyes drift over Rei. "And I'll be watching you," he retorts.

The land begins to change back, getting greener and far more luscious. The capium fields are far behind us now. Midoria slowly comes into view. Metikye is back upfront with Aiden, feeling much better now, but not completely back to himself I assume, for Aiden is still at his side. Roxy and Logan are now beside me.

"Home sweet home," Roxy says.

"You're not from Midoria, are you?" I ask her.

"My caramel skin gives it away?" she asks, amused.

"Sort of, but not really. I...ah...mean..."

She laughs. "Oh, look at you all flustered. Midoria is earth elemental magic centered. If you're not green or married to an earth elemental then you sort of stand out," she says with a chuckle.

"Yes," I nod, relief washing over me.

She smiles. "Yeah, I get that a lot. Aria and Jonathan found me in a bad way twelve years ago. They took me in and gave me a home, and when I was well enough to leave, I couldn't. There was nothing to go back to, so when they invited me to stay, I did. That's when I met Logan here."

We look over to him and he raises his hand to acknowledge us.

"And you, Logan?" I ask.

"Logan doesn't talk much to us and we have been together for years. Don't get upset if you don't get anything from him," Roxy replies on his behalf.

I look over and give Logan a look, but he doesn't give any hint of wanting to say anything. I thought after our long talk we had before that he would talk to me in front of them. They are his friends after all.

I don't want to cause any problems or push the issue, so I simply reply, "I'm happy to of met you all. I'm just grateful you're here."

He lowers his head, trying to hide the blush reddening his face. I think for a moment.

"Logan," I ask, getting his attention. "Did Aria and Jonathan take you in, to?" I ask, trying to make a yes-no question for him.

He nods his head.

"Were you from Midoria originally?"

He shakes his head.

"So, you were with Aria and Jonathan before Roxy?"

He nods.

I think for a moment.

"Logan did you..." I start to ask.

"Look at that everyone!" a voice bellows, distracting me from my question.

We all look up to see the great Medorian kingdom walls towering over us, with two giant doors covered in vines and moss, that creak loudly as they open to welcome us home.

That's strange, I think. *I've been here so short a time, but feel so much more at home here than I ever have in Aiden's kingdom. In a short time here, no one has treated me badly or made me feel unwelcome.*

My andocrit lowers its Giraffe-like legs at the castle steps. A group of people crowd around Rei and me to unload the andocrit of its load. I stand up, gently running my hand over Rei's head, waking her gently. Her eyes flutter open.

"We are here," I say softly.

She opens her mouth with a gigantic yawn, stretches her legs out in front of her, and winces as she does so.

"Be careful," I say quickly.

A scream sounds out. We look over to a couple of maids who have seen Rei and are now losing their minds. I step in front of Rei and rest my face at her cheek. Realizing what I'm doing, she nuzzles me back.

The screams quiet down. Whispers and gasps fly in a wave around us. Paying no attention to their reactions, I keep moving. Logan is already waiting and holds his hand out to me as I walk down off the tattered wing to the ground. Once I'm off, he lifts Rei into the air, placing her down onto a waiting cart gently.

Jonathan and Aria greet us, cautiously sidestepping Rei's cart.

"Well, it looks like you came back with... um...interesting cargo," Jonathan says.

"Please, I'll take care of her. She won't hurt anyone," I say.

"No one will be willing to care for an Akuma, you do realize that?" Jonathan replies.

"Yes of course. I'll stay in a barn with her if I have to."

Aria steps forward "That won't be necessary. Come with me, Bree. Logan, could you bring the Akuma, please?"
Logan nods.

"I can't thank you enough," I say to Aria as we walk.

She sighs. "Are you sure about this Bree?"

"Yes," I say without hesitation.

She takes us to a clearing just behind the castle. I look around, confused. Aria looks at me and smiles. raising her hands. The ground begins to shake and rumble under my feet as the ground begins to shift.

A small seedling pops from the ground and rapidly grows. Reaching higher, it twists and circles, building an incredible foundation. Several more pop from the ground, growing thicker and branching out, making big thick walls to surround the foundation. Aria closes her eyes as a tree grows from the side, reaching out over the building to make a magnificent roof in full bloom with Lillulian's!

"Oh, wow! Aria this is so... Oh my, there are no words for how beautiful this is!" I say enchanted.

She smiles. "I'm glad you like it. This will be your home from now on, whether you decide to stay or just visit. Either way, this is yours."

My mouth drops open as Aiden's arm drops over my shoulders. I look up at him, he doesn't look surprised at all.

"You knew about this?" I ask.

He looks down at me. "Yes, of course. We talked about it before we left. You seem so much happier here, so I thought we would visit a lot at the very least, and I was told nowhere in the castle would be soundproof enough for us, apparently," he grins wickedly.

My face burns a violent blush. Aiden bursts out laughing at me as he guides me inside.

Aria leaves Aiden and I to explore our little mansion on our own. Every part is a work of art, from the main hall to the staircases. It's mind-blowing. We open a door on the top floor, and I gasp. It's a library, a huge library.

"Stick my bed here, I'll never leave!" I say in awe as Aiden chuckles.

"I think our room will be less distracting to you," he growls.

"Aw jealous, are we?" I ask with a smirk.

"I'm jealous of anything that distracts you from me," he admits, swatting my ass.

A little yelp escapes my lips at the sudden contact.

We go through all the rooms until we enter a room where Logan is setting Rei down on a comfy nest-like bed in an exceptionally large bedroom.

"Oh no, she is not staying in our bedroom!" Aiden declares pointedly.

"We can't leave her alone either," I say.

Aiden turns me to him, grabbing my ass in both his hands, giving a little squeeze. My breath hitches.

"Do you really think she will be comfortable in our bedroom?" he says, softly nuzzling into my ear.

I feel his warm breath as he plants a kiss...Oh my god, that damn spot below my ear where my brain turns to mush. Crap, I can't think, and before I know it, I'm devouring Aiden's lips with my own. A thump followed by a whimper brings us both out of the trance we were in.

"Rei!" I gasp and rush to her side. "What were you doing?" I ask, irritated.

She looks at me incredulously. "You can't be serious. I was not going to stay in here for the rest of the show," she says, embarrassed.

"I'm sorry, Rei. Aiden was making a point and I lost. I'm sorry. We will have a different room," I say with a smile.

"No," Aiden and Rei both say at the same time.

I look at them both shocked.

"Until Rei is on her feet, she should not be left alone. I understand that and I'll be on my best behavior while in our room with her here, but I can't make the same promise for the rest of the house," he says with a wicked grin.

Rei rolls her eyes. "Ugh! Okay, okay/ I get it, bedroom safe outside learn to run fast. Got it," she says playfully.

"You need to learn to walk before you can run, Rei," I remark with a smile.

"Just don't make me vomit, I can't get to a good location yet," she remarks.

I giggle.

"We will do our best, but I can't make any promises," Aiden retorts.

I jab him in the side, playfully.

Over the next few days, I go through the steps in my book and extract the fibers and juices from the prillum and petals from the flowers. It's a very long, hard process.

When I have completed everything and all I have left to do is drop the prillum petals in the caldron, I find there is far more than I thought there would be. The recipe will go far with very little, but the good thing is, there is an easy way to preserve the rest for a rainy day.

Word has gotten back to us from Nigalia that all the preparations are underway for our return. The last of the ingredients will be there by the time we get back if we leave in the morning.

I sigh. it's been so nice here I'll really miss it. I walk over to Rei and run my hand over her head and around the back of her right ear. She stirs and stretches as she yawns, but doesn't whimper. I greet her with a smile as her eyes open.

"Good morning, Rei," I say.

"Good morning," She groans greeting me in-kind.

"We will be leaving tomorrow morning for Nigalia," I tell her. "If you're feeling up to it, I think we can get you up and about today. What do you think?" I ask.

She flexes her paws and stretches a bit. "Hmm, I think I might be able to try," she says. Slowly, she puts her heavy weight on her front legs, then slowly pulls her back legs under her.

I look up at her towering over me. "Wow, I forgot how big you are." I say, a little nervous.

She laughs a little and loses her balance for a moment.

"Okay, no laughing until you're much stronger," I say to her.

"Yes, I think you're right."

We walk slowly through the mansion, down the stairs, out the back doors, and into the garden.

"I'm so glad Aria made the house so big, there is no way you would get in and out of a normal size house," I remark.

"Yes, I'm glad, too. The close walls are a great help at keeping me upright as I get used to standing again," she says gratefully.

Out back Aiden is organizing the arrangements for tomorrow's departure. Logan, Roxy, and Metikye are with Aiden. Everyone stops and looks at Rei and I as we walk out. I place my right hand under her chin encouraging her to keep moving.
"I've got you Rei," I say.

She wobbles a little but steadies herself quickly.

I'm thinking of how she must feel, probably the same as I do back in Nigalia. I give her a reassuring pet and press forward.

"I'm here," I say again.

She doesn't say anything, but walks with me.

"Look who is back on her feet," Aiden says. "Looks like I get my bride back from nurse and maid duty," he remarks. Rei and I roll our eyes at him.

"It's a shame we have to leave tomorrow. I know we have to, but I'll miss all of you so much," I say, directing my words at Logan Roxy and Metikye.

"Well, you don't have ta miss us coz we are going with ya," Metikye says with a beaming smile.

I look at Aiden with a look asking if it's true, and he nods at me, smiling.

I bounce on my toes in glee. "Oh, that's wonderful," I squeal. "How long will you be with us for?"

"Aiden has invited us to work with ya, and with losing most of our men and the four that came back, besides Luc, Mac and Nathaniel, all left once we got back. So, we thought we would take the gracious offer to travel with ya for a bit until we decide to move on. If it's all good with ya, that is." He gives me a wink.

"YES! Of course, YES!" I exclaim enthusiastically. Everyone laughs at my excitement as Roxy comes over to me.

"We figured you might be glad for a few friendly faces back home, too," she says with a knowing smile.

"You thought all too right," I say bursting with joy.

"So, are you releasing the Akuma or what?" Mac says, asking the question everyone has been burning to ask me.

I look to Rei, place my hands on her cheeks. "Rei do you want to go home?" I ask.

"Dear child, I have found it wonderful being at your side, but I think I will cause you too much trouble if I stay. I think it's best if I do go," she replies.

I place my head to her forehead looking her dead in the eyes. "I asked you if you WANT to stay or go," I say again.

She shakes her head with a smile in her eyes. "I have no home. I WANT to stay by your side, if you will have me," she says.

"There, was that so hard?" I ask with a satisfied smile. "Rei is a member of our family now. Where we go, she goes," I say authoritatively, waiting for anyone to challenge me, but no one does.

"Okay, let's get everything ready for... Rei, was it?" Roxy asks.

"Yes, Rei is her name," I clarify.

"Okay, then let's get the ride ready for Rei, too. Let's go, people! Move, move, move!" Roxy says, pushing them on with their tasks.

Aiden walks over to me and wraps his arms around my waist. "So, this is really your decision?" Aiden asks.

"Yep," I say without hesitation.

Aiden sighs in my ear. "You better be right about that thing, because if it even looks at you, or anyone else for that matter, in a way I don't like, I'll kill it," he says in a whisper so only I can hear. He presses a kiss to my temple, and walks away.

We said our goodbyes to Aria and Jonathan a couple of days ago and it was much harder than I thought it would be, but having Metikye, Roxy, and the others with me makes leaving the first happy place I've found here a little easier. Aiden said we can go back for a little holiday after everything is dealt with in the kingdom.

Nigalia opens its doors as we approach. The people are lining the path with cheers of our return. It's nice seeing this side of the place. It's so different here, and far less green that I remember. I guess my eyes will have to adjust back from all the green from Midoria. Don't get me wrong, it's green and beautiful here, it's just a big adjustment when you come back.

We approach the castle and I'm ushered out to the kitchens quickly. I look around to find Madeline, but can't find her anywhere. I start making the recipe in a massive cauldron that has been set up for me. One of the requirements of the cure was a cast-iron cauldron with a diamond-dusted finish. I drop the ingredients in and six kitchen hands stir the pot mixing the ingredients.

I drop the prillum into the pot in stages, the fibers first, then after, some plants, roots, and scales, and the juice from the prillum vine. After all the ingredients are in, I give Logan a nod to indicate the cauldron is ready to be transported.

We carefully transport the cauldron to the fields. My barrier is not as strong as I'd left it.

"Looks like we got back in good time," I say, stepping through the barrier. Aiden and Logan try to follow me but are refused entry.

"I'm sorry, but if this goes badly, I need to make sure you are all safe.

Please push the cauldron through to the center as far as you can, Logan. I'll do the rest," I say authoritatively.

"No!" Logan yells.

Everyone gasps. I snap my head to Logan. He doesn't acknowledge anyone's reaction.

"I'm coming with you or you carry it yourself."

I scowl at Logan. He knows damn well he is the only one here who can move that damn thing.

Aiden steps in front of Logan.

"There is no way in hell you're going without me," he barks.

I roll my eyes.

"Logan, come on." Aiden goes to walk through, but my barrier stops him, but lets Logan and the cauldron through.

"Bree! Damn it! I'm coming too, don't you dare!"

I start to walk. "Knowing you're out there safe makes me less nervous," I say as I walk away.

"Damn it, Bree!" Aiden pounds at the barrier. "You're... NOT...LEAV-ING....ME...BEHIND!" he pounds on each word.

I hear a thud and look back to find Aiden face down in the grass, on my side of the barrier. He looks up at me with a grin. I roll my eyes at him and turn back to keep walking.

"Stupid damn bond," I say, sulking under my breath.

I hear Logan laugh and I shoot him a glare. Logan shrugs off with another laugh and a teasing pout.

Aiden must have caught up fast enough to catch what I said because he breathes, "I think it's pretty great," in my ear, making me jump.

When Logan places the cauldron in the center of the infested Lillulian fields, I hold out the open jar that holds the prillum petals and sprinkle a dusting of my magic over them.

The petals begin to glow brightly as Logan lifts them from the jar, gracefully taking them up and dropping them in the cauldron. They hit the surface and it instantly begins to bubble. A thick fog erupts from it.

Not waiting to see what would happen, Aiden grabs my hand and Logan runs with us as fast as our legs can carry us. The fog is close at our heels, moving fast and engulfing everything it passes. We run until we see the others on the other side of the barrier.

We manage to get out just in time, and thank the heavens, my barrier is holding it back. We stay there for a moment just struggling to catch our breath. Once it's easier, we all look back at the barrier to see nothing. The fog is so thick you can't see a thing. Logan, Aiden and I drop to the grass.

"I guess we camp here for the night and wait until it clears to see if the potion worked," Aiden says.

I nod, still breathing heavy. "I hope it works, I know if Madeline was with me it would definitely work, she is brilliant in the kitchen." I say.

Aiden looks at me with shock on his face. "Are you talking about Madeline from the kitchen?" he asks.

"Yes," I say cautiously. "Is she okay?" I ask, getting worried. "Aiden, please, Madeline is my best friend, if anything has happened, you have to tell me," I say urgently.

"Bree, do you remember the night of the ball? There was a crash in the kitchen that pulled me away from you?" he asks.

"How can I forget?" I say dryly.

"There was an explosion that was made with unstable capium crystals, the same substance we found the Lillulian orchards were poisoned with. I'm so sorry, Bree, but Madeline fled the scene that night and no one has seen her since." Aiden says, regretfully.

My heart stops "Madeline? She did all this?" I ask in disbelief.

16

Sky Town

"I can't believe it! There has to be an explanation for all this. We have to do something!" My eyes are welling up and the tightening in my chest won't ease up.

Every moment Madeline and I were together, nothing ever gave me any warnings that she was capable of this. Aiden rests his hands on my shoulders, pulling me to him. I'm too worked up to appreciate the closeness.

"Aiden, please, we have to go after her, find out the truth. She is my best friend, please!" I implore him.

He looks down at me and sighs. "We'll wait until morning, when the fog has cleared and we can see if the cure worked. If not, we need to find another way. The kingdom and its people come first, but if it does work, we'll make sure everything will be set up for us to run things while on the road, that's my offer," he counters.

I sigh. I know he's right. Madeline would be long gone by now, anyway. I nod, not wanting to say anything in case the tears I've been

"

holding back decide to leave me. I'm going to find the truth. Either way, she needs to be found and brought back here for a trial. I have already sent Nathanial after her.

The morning light drifts over us, waking me. My eyes flutter open to the glorious image of Aiden's sleeping face. I smile as I watch his chest rise and fall. His soft lips call to me as he breathes so peacefully. After all we have been through, I'm sure he's exhausted. I lift my head a little more to see him better when his eyes open.

"How long have you been watching me?" he asks with a smirk.

"Not long enough, go back to sleep," I say, raising my hand to his face.

He catches my wrist and flips himself over on top of me, pinning me down. "I can think of better things to do than sleep," Aiden grins, lowering his face to mine.

"Ahem, please, remember half the kingdom is here." Aiden and I look over to where Roxy is, straightening out her clothes. Aiden looks back at me, remembering where we are. I smile apologetically. Aiden sighs and moves off me.

"Okay, the fog has gone. Let's see if it worked," Roxy says.

We all get up and move to my now very weak barrier. It held up better than I thought it would, for my first time at least.

"I think I should go first before I take it down altogether," I suggest.

Aiden walks next to me. "We go together, I don't think this will last much longer anyway."

I sigh, raising my hand to the barrier. It dissipates in a light mist, letting all of us move forward through the orchard. The smiles spread wider, and wider on all the faces around us as we walk further. No one says a thing. The lack of capium is overwhelming, but no one makes a sound as we walk, looking for the tiniest piece, afraid if we make a sound the hopes would be shattered. We get through to the very end before everyone erupts into cheers.

"It's cured!" someone shouts.

"It worked!" says someone else.

Everyone lifts me into the air, and carries me through town, cheering and spreading the news. The orchard is cured and the capium is gone. News travels fast and the kingdom is in a full swing celebration. I'm let down at the castle steps, where Aiden stands waiting for me, a proud smile on his face.

Early the next morning, Aiden wakes me with kisses all over my body. "Mmmmm, that feels good," I say appreciatively, tangling my fingers in his hair.

"How do you feel?" he asks me a little concerned.

Content I admit "Good, a bit sore but good,"

"That's good, I was worried I overdid it with you last night," he says into my stomach.

I lift his head up to look at me. "You didn't overdo anything. I needed last night just as much as you, and I don't remember complaining one bit," I say with a grin, stretching out and pushing my body seductively into his chest.

Aiden grins widely, a growl rolling through his throat as he prowls up my body to kiss me. Just as his lips touch mine, there is a knock at the door.

"Are you kidding me!" Aiden huffs at the closed-door. "What is it!" he snaps loudly.

"I...I have an urgent message... from Nathaniel." A panicked voice stammers through the door.

Aiden snatches a blanket from the bed and wraps it around himself. He flings the door open, grabs the message, and slams the door closed in the terrified maid's face.

"What is it?" I ask as I look at Aiden's face change.

"It's Nathaniel. His note says,

Get everyone to Sky Town as soon as possible!
Nathaniel."

I'm packing our bags for our trip to Sky Town, which is not that hard as we never unpacked, but I do change some things over and repack to fit others, when Rei comes into the room.

"So, we are off again?" she asks.

"Yes, WE are off. YOU are not," I state.

"What! You can't leave me behind," she barks.

"No, Aiden said Sky Town is going to be too rough on you, you're better off staying here," I reply.

"I'm going with you!" She declares, challenging me.

"No way, most of the kingdoms will run in terror once they see you, Rei. You're not coming, and that's final," I say.

Rei stands before me in a challenging stance.

"If that's so true, you can't leave me behind either. Without you, no one will care for me once you're gone. Either way, you have to take me and you know it!" she argues back.

Damn, she is right, I hadn't thought of that, I sigh. I look to Rei who seems pleased with herself now. I'm guessing from the look on my face she thinks she has won, and I know it to be true. Then a thought strikes me.

I run to my bag and pull out my book. I fling it open and flick wildly for the page I need. "Where is it?" I scold myself. "GOT IT!" I say way too loudly, startling Rei. I walk to her with a wide grin. "Okay, you want to go so bad? That's fine, you can go, but not as you are," I say smugly.

Rei raises a crystal eyebrow at me as I turn the page to her. Her eyes grow wide. "Oh, no you don't! You're not using that on me," she says, scrambling for the door.

"Oh, come on. Everyone will be happy with this," I say with a smile.

"Not me!" she growls.

"Oh, come on. You're acting like a Frady chittle," I say, with amusement.

"Oh, take that back! I'm not afraid!" she says, defensively.

"Then what's the harm?" I ask.

She sighs. "Will it hurt?" she asks.

"No, not if I do it right," I remark cheekily.

She scowls at me. "You better do it right, then," Rei replies through gritted teeth.

"It's just an illusion. Only light magic will be able to see through it. Now all I have to do is think of something to disguise you as. Oh, I've got it!" I cry out.

"If it's a chittle, I will eat you," she grumbles.

I giggle. "It's not, I promise, and while you were complaining, I already did it," I sass.

"What? That easy?" she asks.

"Yep, that easy," I retort with a smile. "Look in the mirror, you can see for yourself." I rock on my heels gleefully.

Rei moves to the mirror to see her reflection. What in the name of magic? Rei's illusion form is of a Bupper puppy. She is covered in soft, fluffy, white fur with silver tinsel-like streaks that shimmer. Her ears are tall on her head like a bunny, and her tail is long and elegant.

"Oh, wow! You look so adorable. No one is going to be able to keep their hands off you," I say beaming.

"They better! It's just an illusion, remember," She growls.

"Yes, it is, one that will stay as long as I'm alive or remove it myself." I say with glee.

"What made you come up with this form?" Rei asks me thoughtfully examining her reflection.

"It's one of the first creatures Aiden introduced me to a long time ago," I say remembering the moment when we were kids. "Oh, um, the memory just popped to mind, that's all, why do you ask? I think it's perfect."
"No reason I was just not expecting it that is all" she replies.

Quietly I watch her examining herself for a moment, shaking off the strange feeling "Come on, Rei, let's go," I say ushering her out the door.

We meet Aiden outside, where he is setting up for the trip. Luc and Mac are arguing prices for supplies, and Roxy is checking crates. Logan is loading up after Roxy gives him the go-ahead.

Metikye is keeping everyone on their tasks, and where they're supposed to be. Nathaniel still hasn't been seen yet but if anyone can find Madeleine's trail, it's him. I notice something that confuses me. I walk over to Aiden.
"Why is everything being set up into one? It looks like a big box like a bus with no wheels," I observe.

"This is how we are traveling," he tells me.

"What is possibly big enough to carry that on its own?"

Aiden smiles at me as he points in the air.

I look up and my mouth falls open. It's a freaking whale with wings! Its massive shadow slowly moves over the castle.

"When it comes over us, we send these cables up, locking onto the anchor points at eight different sections of the harnesses around the Oregrin. We are a small cargo in comparison to what it usually carries," Aiden says simply.

We all get into the packed bus carriage. As Logan lifts the cables up and the loud clink sounds, and the hooks snap in place at all eight points of the harness around the Oregrin.

"Okay, all secured. Take us up," Metikye calls.

One big yank lurches everyone and up. We hear loud woosh sounds with each beat of the Oregrin's wings. A gentle rub of Aiden's fingers to my arm brings me around from my sleep.
"Are we there?" I ask sleepily.

"No, but I didn't think you wanted to miss this," Aiden says with a gentile hum.

I sit up and look out the window. My heart is pounding out of my chest. I am very much awake now. There are floating islands all around us. It takes me a while to realize there are hundreds of these islands all circling one massive platform, and on it stands a magnificent statue, bigger than any tower I have ever seen.

The statue is of a breathtaking beauty. Her head is back, looking up. Both her hands are reaching to the sky, and her long hair falls down her back, meeting her long flowing dress. The platform has a cascade of waterfalls all around it, falling to the empty space below.

"Wow!" I say.

Aiden looks at me as I'm awestruck. "You see where the maiden is holding her hands up?" Aiden asks.

"Yes, she is kind of hard to miss," I giggle.

Aiden smiles back. "I don't mean that. If you look closely as we approach, you will see she is holding her hands up to the entrance to Aquilla, the land of water elementals. They are said to be the wisest of all. It's unheard of to be accepted through the door. There are several legends of what the maiden represents," Aiden reveals.

"Like what?" I ask, excitedly intrigued.

"Some say she holds up the world and it would collapse if not for her. Some say she is a beacon for those lost. Some say she is the gate-keeper for a legend that could be the greatest blessing the lands will ever know, or the end of all we know."

"What do you believe?" I ask.

"Me? I believe all of them to be true," Aiden says with a shrug.

I look into her face as we pass. My heart sinks. The look on her face is painful to see. Her expression is one of holding the weight of the world, a protector, even if it destroys her. A tear escapes as we pass and I see the two waterfalls falling from her eyes. She is crying, but her tears are flowing up to the swirling whirlpool above. I jump when Aiden wipes my tear away.

"It's just stories, Bree," he says soothingly.

"I know, it's just seeing her like this really affects me. I can feel all her heartache, it's all over every inch of her," I say, breaking away and burying my face into Aiden's chest. "So, is this Sky Town?" I ask, trying to change the subject.

"No, this is called the in-between. You can't land anywhere here, but the outer islands are for-profits and those of faith. It's a very sacred place. This is where sky meets water. The Skylands and Aquilla both coexist like two magnets pushing each other away, holding a perfect balance," he says.

A couple of hours later we arrive in Sky Town. My mind is full of everything I have seen and heard. It's only when we hear a loud thud that bumps and jerks everyone forward that I come back from my thoughts.

Logan and Metikye are unhooking the Oregrin and unloading everything. I lose my footing as I step out. I gasp, the edge is so close I can't see the ground. It takes me a moment to realize Aiden had grabbed my arm when I tripped.

"Be careful, it's a long way down if you fall," he snips, pulling me back from the edge.

"Glad you finally made it." We snap our heads to the voice.

"Nathaniel."

Aiden walks over to him and I follow.

"We were getting worried about you. No word at all, then a note to meet you here with the team and that's it. We thought the worst!" I say waving my hands about like a crazy person.

Nathaniel pulls me into a hug. "Awe, you was wowied about me," he says, lifting me like a child would a cat.

Aiden seems amused at my annoyance of the playful banter and baby talk at my expense. I shoot a look to Nathaniel, who stops and puts me down abruptly, holding his hands up in surrender.

"Okay, okay. I'm sorry. Aiden knows how I work. It's how I get results and I did, she is here," Nathaniel explains, defensively.

"Do you mean Madeline?" I ask in excitement.

"Yes, she was last spotted at a tavern two stones over," he says pointing down a cobbled road.

Not waiting for the others, I race down the stone streets passing home after home. They all sit on top of a small twister and there is nothing on the ground but a welcome mat. *I'll ask questions about that after,* I think, pressing on.

I'm out of breath by the time I get to the tavern. I stop at the entrance, my lungs burning as I struggle to breathe normally. I can't wait, I need answers now. I step forward and open the door. I look around the tavern and my heart sinks, she isn't here.

"Madeline, where are you?" I sink into a dark booth off to the side and throw my face in my hands.

"My dear, sweet Bree, what are you doing here?"

That voice.... I lift my head and launch myself at Madeline. She gasps but catches me. I hold her tightly to me as I sob.

"You missed me that much?" she asks, while stroking my hair.

"Please, tell me everything they are saying is all lies," I beg, lifting my face to look at her.

She looks into my pleading eyes and sighs, releasing me.

"No, it can't be," I say in disbelief.

She looks at the floor for a moment, until she raises her face to look at me. "It's not what you think, Bree, I promise. You need to trust me," she implores, so quiet it's almost a whisper.

The door bursts open as Aiden and the others file into the tavern. Madeline bolts across the room, jumping behind the bar and out the back. I run after her, weaving through baskets and boxes to the back door. I follow as fast as I can. Damn, she is fast.

I'm doing my best just to keep her in my sights when something leaps past me and thunders towards Madeline, leaping and knocking her to the ground. Madeline flips over to see her assailant.

"ENOUGH!" Rei barks over her.

Madeline stops thrashing immediately, frozen under Rei. "Is it you?" Madeline gasps.

"Yes, now stop this," Rei says, more calmly this time.

"You look different," Madeline says, confused.

"Yes, Bree put an illusion over me to make it easier to move around without upsetting the locals."

Madeline's mouth drops open. "Bree knows?" she asks.

Rei shakes her head.

"Oh, I see. Well, ridiculously cute disguise," she laughs.

"Enough," she warns.

All Madeline manages is to laugh through her lips. Rei rolls her eyes and sighs.

"What is going on here? How do you know each other?" I blurt out.

Rei lets Madeline up as Aiden and the others catch up to us. They're all at my side looking as baffled as I am. Rei senses this, and turns to face us.

"I think it's time you knew what you were up against, and Madeline is going to tell you all," announces Rei.

"Are you sure?" she asks Rei.

"Yes, but not here. Is there someplace private we can go?"

"Sure is, follow me," Madeline says, leading the way.

Madeline weaves us through the roads, and across island after island, with terrifying airlifts, I really don't care for at all. When we reach a small island with nothing but a big tree....

"A treehouse?" I say out loud.

Madeline looks at me and smiles. "Yep, home sweet home." She pulls a vine, and a ladder falls for us to climb up to a veranda. It's beautiful and goes round the entire house. I have to admit it has an incredible view and is very spacious inside.

We all settle down on her couch and wait for Madeline to talk. After an uncomfortable stretch of silence, Rei clears her throat and Madeline sits to attention and starts to talk.

"Okay, let's start with...yes, I was responsible for the explosion in the kitchen at the ball, but that was an accident. That snooping Angela grabbed my bag, trying to see what I didn't want her to see. When we were struggling one of the vials with raw material, it flew out of my bag and smashed to the ground. It exploded, sending almost every-one flying.

Thank goodness no one was seriously hurt, but I grabbed my bag and left as fast as I could. I ran to the orchard, knowing that incident took my last bit of time I had. I used the vial I had made and hoped it would work. Then I left that night," she says breathless.

"Why would you do that?" we all ask, pretty much in unison.

Madeline looks to Rei and sighs. "Because the king is not the king, he is an imposter."

Everyone but Aiden and I draw in a breath, but don't say anything. Madeline continues.

"Aiden, I have served your family since I was a child,"

"I know, you were always with my mother until that day," Aiden says, lowering his eyes to the floor.

"Aiden, what you think isn't exactly what happened."

Aiden looks up at her.

"The day it all fell...Bree's father stabbed your mother in the chest," She says quietly.

"I know, I watched her fall to the ground," he hisses in annoyance.

Madeline sighs in defeat. "Reina, this is just too hard to say," Madeline says to Rei.

Aiden's eyes widen. Rei looks to Aiden and places a massive paw on his knee.

"Yes, son it's me."

17

A Heart Worthy Of A Queen

"Mother?" Aiden asks wide-eyed.

"Yes," she says with a smile.

"I... but I saw you get stabbed! How are you...this?" Aiden gestures to her appearance.

"It's a long story. I'm happy to tell you, but please give me a chance to explain."

Aiden closes his mouth and watches Reina.

"I was given warning Verillia were coming for us. After I told your father, all the kingdoms came together to attack Verillia first. That day, the battle separated many of us, and I from your father. I kept a dagger that was given to me, with a special purpose. I searched everywhere for your father to give it to him. I never got to him before I was attacked. King Kintarbie knocked me to the ground, and the blade fell from my hand. I tried to get to the dagger before he could... but I failed. He picked it up and thrust it into my chest." Reina winces as she remembers.

"The dagger was coated with a capium poison that was meant to kill Kintarbie, but when I saw you crossing swords with him, I took the chance when the explosion went off, to run at him, sending us both out the window. I remember waking up down the stream in the morning. That's where Madeline's scream woke me," she says, shuddering.

"You try fetching water and finding an Akuma OUTSIDE the capium fields."

Reina rolls her eyes and continues. "Yes, well, as you can gather, I looked like this. I explained to Madeline what had happened, and it so happened Madeline was in the woods that night where she saw Kintarbie cast the illusion on himself before setting your father in crystal. We have been working together ever since."

"What is going on?" Logan asks getting up. "We are not of Nigalia, we can't understand what she is saying."

Madeline gets up ushering everyone outside. "I'll catch you all up, let's leave them for a bit."

"Would you prefer if I go, too?" I ask.

"No, child. Please stay. You understand me fine," Reina says. "I've wondered why for a while now, but I believe it to be true. You two are bound, aren't you?"

Aiden looks at me with a twinkle in his eyes, taking my hand in his. "Yes, mother," he says with pride.

She smiles a big smile. "I'm so happy for you. I thought I would never see a true bond in my lifetime, but here you are, my son," she says, with equally as much pride. "I have been following Kintarbie as best as I can. He's definitely up to something. I don't know where your father is, but I know he has him somewhere in the far reaches of Verillia. That's where he's been traveling to ever since Bree came back," she exclaims.

"Came back? You know?" Aiden and I say at the same time.

"Oh, you two were never very good at keeping away from each other," she says with a laugh. "The first time you two met I was picking Lillulian's in the orchard with Aiden. A bright blue light filled the orchard. As fast as it had appeared it was gone. That's when I heard Aiden scream. He had fallen into the river that split the orchard. I dropped my basket and ran to Aiden as fast as I could, but when I got there, this sweet little girl was there. She made a rope appear in a flash of blue light and threw it to my son, pulling him to safety," Reina says fondly. "Once Aiden was out of the water, she stayed by his side, making sure he was okay. I thought it best to stand back and see what would happen."

"You are light magic, and I couldn't believe you would save someone not your own kind, but as I watched the two of you, I saw you were not what I expected.

So, when you kept meeting up, I didn't say anything. I thought having someone of light magic would be good, especially one so young and innocent. They would know that we are not the monsters they make us out to be. I made sure it was all kept quiet and no one got in your way when you were together," Reina says.

Aiden and I look at each other in shock. "We thought no one knew!" Aiden and I say in unison.

"Oh, no one knew besides me. One maid spotted Aiden sneaking out of his room late one night but that was it. My husband didn't even know. As long as no one was getting hurt, I didn't see the harm, and I didn't want the fuss that came with explaining Aiden was safe with someone of light magic.

The night Aiden disappeared frightened me. I was so worried, but when he came home, I was relieved but when I caught him climbing through his window. I told Aiden not to sneak out at night anymore, and when he replied it would never happen again, I was concerned. After that, it got worse. Aiden stopped going out. He stayed by his father a lot more and he stopped laughing. Then I found out King Kintarbie's only daughter went missing around the same time.

I didn't have a clue you were the princess. When you disappeared, Bree, your father went mad storming all the kingdoms searching for you. No one knew a thing about what happened, and I never had the courage to voice my suspicions that the last person to see you was my very own son," she admits quietly.

I look to Aiden. "He was the last person here to see me, but I don't know why he did what he did. Even with our bond, it's never been revealed to me," I say, not taking my eyes off him.

Aiden sighs. "I snuck over to the castle to see you one day. When you didn't meet with me, I was worried. When I was sneaking through to your room, I came across a room where I overheard your father talking to a man he called 'brother'. Bree, they were talking about taking you to the in-between maiden!" Aiden exclaims. "Even though I was just a boy, I knew that was a death sentence. I'd rather you gone but safe, than dead," he says, as tears threaten his eyes.

"I don't know what is going on, but I do remember things that terrify me of that man, and my uncle killed my mother right in front of my eyes," I say angrily. "If it was you, I would have done the same," I say.

Aiden wraps his arms around me in relief.

"What happened? Where did you go for all this time?" Reina asks curiously.

"We were asking you what was going on? You're an Akuma and you had Madeline poison our fields and blow up our kitchen without good reason. We still have to take her back," Aiden says.

Reina sighs. "The field was to force Kintarbie's hand to find a cure, so I could get a cure for this," she gestures to her form. "But he didn't do a damn thing! It was all Bree. I followed everywhere you both went, trying to keep you safe in the shadows. When the Akuma attacked, I tried to intervene, but I ended up getting flung into a bush instead," she winces.

"I am sorry, we did not know and if it wasn't for Bree...oh, no!" Aiden realizes. "I almost killed you!" he shouts.

"Aiden, it is okay. You were protecting the one you love, and I am not exactly standing out as your mother right now," she chuckles.

"It is not funny. If Bree was not there, I could have..." he starts.

"But you didn't. We are all here now, together, getting long-awaited answers," Reina interjects.

"Okay, the good thing is, Kintarbie hasn't seen you yet. He's been away on business a lot, so our trips have been mostly unnoticed. He probably has informants, but we have had good reason for what we have done so far, so we need to go back and find out why he's so desperate to give Bree's life to the maiden," Aiden says.

Reina looks at us. "It is said that only the heart of a worthy queen can stand before the maiden. If he takes Bree to the maiden, it is for one reason. He believes Bree to be worthy of judgment. If she has such a heart, the maiden will judge her, but all who have stood before the maiden until now have all perished," Reina says, sounding a little worried.

18

Worlds Will Fall

"No, I can't be! If I face the maiden I... I can't... I won't!" I say in a panic.

"None of this makes sense. I lost my mother for this? You couldn't face the maiden as a child, they had to wait for you to be older." Aiden says.

"A maiden you mean?" I snip.

"Yes!" Reina says.

"So, me sending her away did nothing? Her magic called her back when it was close to the time?" Aiden asks.

"Yes, I believe so. We can't let Kintarbie get his hands on her," Reina says, unhappy with the situation.

"We need to get Bree as far away as possible. She can't go back where he can get his hands on her," Aiden barks.

"I agree," Reina replies.

"Okay, let's get the others and fill them in. They all love you, Bree. None of them would let anything happen to you," Aiden says, trying to assure me.

"I appreciate all this, I do, but we still have to get the leftover ingredients I have stashed away in our room so we can try the cure on Reina. You said it yourself, the lillulian poisoning was a way to find a cure for you and we did."

"Yes, that was the plan, but your safety is more important right now," Reina replies.

We move outside to the veranda. It's dark out now. I can't see anything. The silence sends a chill down my spine. "Madeline, Metikye, Roxy? Where are you? Nathaniel, Logan, Mac, Luc?" I call out to each of my friends in the darkness.

I climb down the ladder, but before my foot touches the ground, a hand wraps around my mouth, pulling me off the ladder. Another hand thrusts a dagger to my throat.

"BREE!" Aiden yells.

The light from the dagger shows my attacker is of light magic. The light illuminates the dark just enough to see my friends tied up and unconscious on the ground.

"My dear, sweet niece, I think it best for your friends here if you come with me quietly," the voice hisses into my ear.

My blood runs cold. *He said niece! My uncle!* I nod, giving him the answer, he was waiting for.

"What a good girl. I taught you well."

"NO!" Aiden thunders from the verandah. "YOU'RE NOT TAKING HER!"

With one wicked grin from my uncle at Aiden, we vanish in a flash of blue light.

When the light fades, we are standing in a large field dotted with glowing, blue bugs that are flying all around us. I look closer. They're just heads with big feet and transparent wings. Their long hair flows around them as they fly. If I wasn't so scared, I think it would be beautiful. My uncle grabs me by the arm, and tugs me harshly towards the massive castle ahead.

"Not the time to play with Jubes, girl," he says, tugging me harder.

The castle looks run down, with bricks missing in places. We approach the thick, heavy front doors that look like the only new thing about it. The door opens as my uncle raises his dagger in the air. He steps forward, dragging me in front of him, then gives me a shove through the doors.

I feel the blade pressed to my back and know I'm meant to keep walking if I don't want it to become a part of me. I know this man and how he treats so-called 'family'. We walk the halls, and it's cold and dark. The pictures are broken, or burned in places, and banners that adorn the walls are ripped and shabby.

We enter a large room with a massive stone table. Hundreds of people sit lining each side of it, and at the very top, in a grand throne chair, sits my father.

"How wonderful for you to join us," he booms with a hearty laugh. "Please, come sit here next to me." He pats the seat next to him. Although I've seen this man all along, it feels different now I know the truth.

I sit quietly next to my father as he waves a hand for a plate of food to be placed in front of me and my glass filled. He raises his glass to the room.

"Here's to finally being altogether," he says, with a deep boom of delight.

The entire room stands and raises their glasses. Everyone falls silent, waiting for me to rise and do the same. The smile doesn't leave my father's face. There is a lot of chatter after the toast. Feeling a stare boring into me, I look over to see my father looking at me.

"I'm sorry to bring you here like this. I had hoped you would come to me on your own and we would travel here together."

I stay quiet as he continues.

"I had hoped you would ask more questions about the book I gave you and open the lines of discussion more, but you kept disappearing each day, and bumping into you got harder as you spent more and more time at that tree," he grumbles.

"How did you know about that?" I ask.

He smiles. "The same way I found you in Sky Town," he answers.

"And how was that?" I ask.

"The book I gave you. The stone on the front cover is how I always know where you are," he admits as if it is the most natural thing to do.

Well, I'll be smashing that the first chance I get, I think to myself.

He waits for a few beats to see if I have anything to say. "When did you get back your memories, Bree?" my father asks me.

"I don't have all my memories back, but I started remembering shortly after I got the book," I say, not wanting him to know they started returning because of Aiden.

He smiles. "The book, was it? I doubt that very much. It was that boy, wasn't it?" he asks.

I snap my head to look at him, eyes wide. "What do you mean?" I stammer.

"I know you and Aiden have a real bond. It took a while to figure it out, but a boy was seen sneaking you back into the castle one night when you were young," he says. "I was so furious. My wife took you from me that night. She was terrified I would take you to the maiden early, fearing I might think you would lose your way. Aiden was that boy, wasn't he?"

I stay quiet. Seeing my refusal to answer, he continues.

"Not that it matters now, anyway. I got you back only to lose you again, but finding you were bonded was the best thing to have happened. Truly, I am elated." he gushes.

"How so?" I ask in disgust.

He laughs at my obvious disdain. "The prophecy says a maiden heart worthy of a queen, with magic not of this land would stand before the gatekeeper and be judged, removing all magic of this land," he recites.

"If all magic is removed from this land, you will be powerless to," I spit.

He moves in closer. A smile that chills me to the bone crosses his face. "Magic not of this land. Only this land's magic will be gone. Our magic is not of this land." he laughs.

My brows furrow at this concept. "What do you mean, I'm not from here?" I ask.

"Oh, yes, you are of this land, Bree, but our magic was brought here from another land. Therefore, it will survive while the rest dies," he states calmly.

"But that will destroy everything. The creatures of magic will die, the sky lands will fall, Aquilla will be destroyed and flood most of the lands, without magic...."

"Yes, Bree, worlds will fall. Not just this one, but all others connected to this one, too," he agrees, adding to the already bad situation.

"How could you want that?" I gasp indignantly.

"For years I have waited for this day. The moment you came back I knew now is the time. My child will finally put things back as they should be," he exclaims with pride.

"How could you think I would help you?" I ask.
"You have no choice. Thanks to your mother, you are drawn to the truth. Only you will make the future better. Your bond is key. When you stand before the maiden, you will be judged as a queen. Your heart

has been judged already to be bound, and is stronger for it, too. When you are judged, that is when it will begin, the draining of the world's magic," he scoffs. "Tomorrow night when the moon is high, we will take you to the in-between."

"I will fight you with everything I have! I'll stop you from hurting these people!" I seethe.

"Oh, Bree, you have gotten much stronger, but you have not even scratched the surface of what we are capable of," he states, amusement spreading across his face.

I look at my untouched plate and push some vegetables around on it. My deerling knocks my glass over trying to have a drink, but not liking the taste. I giggle.

"Where did you come from?" I say.

My father laughs. "Well, your deerling is really something," he says with pride.

"Isn't everyone's the same?" I ask, a little taken back.

"No, they're most definitely not." He calls his own. Its light is no-where near as bright as mine, and it's older, and shabby looking, and nowhere near as active as mine.

"Our deerlings are connected to our magic, simply a training tool, but yours is connected to your heart, it seems, making it bright and vibrant. Yours has something I've never seen before. It has a life of its own. When you first called it, the deerling was different, wasn't it?"

I nod.

"And over time it just started doing things on its own?"

Again, I nod.

"This was while you were alone, but as you began to make friends, your deerling appeared less and less, am I right?"

I nod, slowly realizing this all to be true.

He claps his hands together as a gleeful laugh leaves him. "Oh Bree, you have not disappointed me at all. When you disappeared, I searched everywhere for you, but the day Nigalia attacked us, I felt your presence. When Aiden's blade crossed with mine, I shared your bond with him for just a moment, and I knew what had happened. I knew he was the boy you were seen with that night. I knew you were alive and I knew how to bring you home," he declares.

"YOU! You sent the Akuma after me, didn't you?!" I accuse.

My father leans back in his chair linking his fingers together in front of his chest. "Yes, I did." he says calmly.

"That thing almost killed me, and it could have hurt my niece!"

He throws himself forward, pounding his hands to the table, making me jump. My deerling scatters behind my bowl. "THEY are not your family. WE are and you never belonged there! You needed to be put in a position to awaken your power and light your way home to us!" he yells.

"I was given that life because the people who really cared about me tried to keep me safe from MY family!" I thunder back.

The room has gone quiet now, and my deerling is hiding in my bowl amongst my noodles.

"You think they ever really cared about you? Don't make me laugh! They wanted to get to us, through you, taking a poor sweet, stupid child down to ensure they will still have power," he sneers.

"THAT'S NOT TRUE!" I scream at him.

"Oh, really? Did any of them tell you about the prophecy?" he asks.

"No, not exactly," I admit. "But they did say all who have been taken there die."

"That is true because they did not meet all that was required. They all knew that magic would be taken from this world and all those connected to it the moment the chosen one stood before the maiden," he admits to me.

"There has to be a reason why they didn't tell me," I wonder out loud.

19

Never Give Up On Me

I was led to a rather nice room, considering the state of the rest of the castle, but as I understand, since the cloaking enchantment was put up around the perimeter to keep it looking abandoned some repairs have started on the castle. I know this was my room before. Even though it is lovely, and it does not have the musty smell most of the other rooms have, it feels cold and lonely here.

Looking towards the window on the far side of the room, I go to walk over to see if it will open so I can find a way out, but as I do so, my deerling jumps up on the window sill and immediately gets flung across the room in a flash. I rush over to see if it's all right. By the time I get over to where he landed, my deerling has already shaken off the blast and is determined to go again. I laugh as I catch him in mid-air.

"Oh, no you don't!" I say, giving him a pat to distract him. "It looks like the castle has a barrier around it. We can casually look around and see, what do you say?"

My deerling peeps and vibrates a purr.

"How adorable can you be?" I ask lovingly. While playing with my deerling, I go out the bedroom door. "Hmm, that's interesting. I'm not locked in my room so that's a good sign. Reina said King Darnell was encased in crystal with my father. I wonder if we can find where my father is keeping him?" I say to my deerling.

My deerling is not listening to me as I pet him. I wander down the long, dark hall only illuminated by the light of my deerling. The further I walk, the mustier and colder it gets.

"Well, it looks like this part is still untouched," I murmur to myself.

I enter a few rooms that are either a mess of broken furniture and smolder marks, or the furniture is covered in sheets and the room is filled with cobwebs. Room after room, they're much the same, until I reach the last door. This room is a mixture of both. I lift a sheet from the right-side wall to find a dresser with neat brushes and combs with beautiful handles of flowers in resin.

These are flowers from my world. I look at them closely, confused. *How is this here?* I look around the room more. The floor in the middle is covered in smashed furniture, not like the others.

This looks like the room was broken apart in a fit of rage. Only the dresser and a large wooden box with beautiful carvings all over it of butterflies, they look like the starlight butterfly I saw in the garden with Aiden.

The lock on the front of it is old. I go to touch it, when a voice from behind me makes me jump. My deerling falls from my hand. It was in the middle of rubbing his side on my thumb when I jumped, causing him to roll off my palm.

"I'm sorry father, was I not allowed in here?" I ask, trying to keep my composure.

"I'm sorry if I startled you. I just like to wander when I can't sleep. I assume that is your issue, too?" he asks me.

I nod. "I know this room," I say quietly.

"Yes, you would. This was your mothers' room and your nursery a long time ago," he replies.

"Everything in here is broken, except for the box and dresser," I say as calm as I can.

"Yes, I came in here the night after you and your mother where taken from me. I did a little...remodeling. I'm not proud, but I never could bring myself to fix it or get rid of it. You probably think it's silly, right?" he asks me with a hint of embarrassment in his tone.

"Not really. You left the dresser untouched for a reason, didn't you?" I ask him knowingly.

"I saw her here most at that dresser," he remarks.

"Do you miss her?" I ask hopefully.

"Yes, I do, every moment of every day," he admits.

"Then why do you have that man...my uncle at your side?" I choke out, hating the words every time I say them.

"All though he does not have light magic, he has been very useful to the cause," he replies.

"Hang on, I've seen him use light magic every time I remember him."

"Ah yes, he can only use a little magic that I've put into that dagger of his. Without it, he can't do anything. It was the same with my late wife and her wedding ring. In fact, the only two people left who can use light magic are you and I. The rest of our people use items infused with my light magic."

I think on this for a moment. Each time I remember, he has had that blade. "That's how he got to mum," I say, in almost a whisper.

"Yes, I gave him the tools to find you. I thought his desire to strip the lands of power was enough for him, but I underestimated how much he hated her," he says, breathing out a deep sigh.

I turn from him, not wanting to meet his gaze. The thought makes me sick to my stomach. "If he hates magic so much, why is he helping you?" I challenge.

"He was only too happy to help me strip the lands of magic and give him the power to do it. That desire is immensely powerful, and makes for a good loyal supporter, don't you think?" my father replies in a tone suggesting he should not have had to explain that one.

"You got him to kill your own wife and plan on doing the same to your only daughter," I spit, my every word dripping with disdain.

"I have absolutely no plans for you to be killed!" he snaps.

I'm taken back at seeing him lose his temper. I keep my mouth shut and listen.

"I never told him to kill her, it just happened that way. I never knew his hate for her would out way his desire to rid magic. I knew from the very beginning that she never loved me. Our marriage was one of mutual arrangement, her family needed my help to survive and I needed a bride." She knew I could never love her, for my heart was lost long ago, so our arrangement was perfect, but she found peace when she gave her heart to another. The day I heard she had died, I honestly didn't think it would affect me, but in some way, it did. All I asked was that he bring you back at any cost, that cost was, unfortunately, her life," he sighs, clearly upset. "A shame really, I loved how she loved you, at least...."he shakes his head as if getting rid of an unwanted thought.

"I have told people only what they need to know, nothing more. What must be done is only for you, me, and the maiden to know. I have never lied to you. I have been myself from the beginning with you, there were no illusions. You are destined to right a wrong from long ago. I am truly sorry you have any part in it, but this is the only way...." he starts to say, once again, he drifts off into thought after a few moments he realizes this. "You should get some rest. We will set out at first light to make it to the maiden for when the moon is high." Without another word, he turns and leaves.

'Cold, heartless bastard' is the only thing raging in my head the entire time I walk back to my room. He didn't stop smiling throughout most of that talk. On top of that, I searched all the rooms and didn't find a thing as to where King Darnell could be. My father didn't even seem phased that I was looking around. The thought infuriates me further.

I think about my mother and all that was said. *Who was it my mother fell in love with that gave her peace? How do I process my father and I are the only ones with natural light magic? Is it the truth? He did say he hasn't lied to me and as far as I can remember he hasn't, keeping things from me is not lying but the main thing that perplexes me is he spoke fondly of my mother one moment then didn't seem to care much the next.*

At some point my exhaustion gets the better of me and I fall asleep.

We have been traveling for most of the day. We set out at first light this morning, and the trip has not been anywhere near as enjoyable as the ones with Aiden, I sigh as I pull at the side of the uncomfortable white cloth dress they shoved me into. the sleeves are long and flair out, at the wrists, and a cloak and oversized hood are semi-attached to the dress, all though very pure and godly looking it may be, it is uncomfortable as hell, making me wish I was back in my brown leather pants and white off the shoulder shirt I'm use to.

I look out the carriage and can't see much, as people on andocrits and crolldars are all around us blocking out most of the view. The crolldar next to me is half the size of an andocrit but still the size of two Clydesdale horses. Its skin is like a crocodile with no tail, but fat with horns like a rhino. We hear a loud commotion up ahead and the carriage comes to an abrupt halt.

"What is going on?" my father barks in annoyance.

"Your Highness, you should come and see this," one of the men calls down from an andocrit.

We step out and walk to the edge of a cliff. It drops down into a valley we need to go through to get to the maiden on the other side.

"Why can't we just port there?" I ask, cocking my head to the side.

My father smiles. "The maiden protects all of the in-between from all kinds of magic and none of our group can port, even if we could, because they don't have natural light magic."

I think this over for a moment. It seems even I can't port, since I have failed every time I have tried. I don't know if it's this place or if my father has done something to prevent me. Since I have tried many times before we got here, I feel it is most likely my father.

I look out over the vast space and see a large valley at the bottom covered in a mass of people. This is a battlefield. The lands have come together to save, not just our world, but all the worlds, to stop me from being delivered to the maiden. My heart pulls at the thought of all that I love being down there. *Are they here to destroy me or save me?* My father's words ring through my head more, if that is even possible.

They do care for me. They can't risk that someday I would decide to destroy all magic. I wish I could just go back to Mia, Tom, and the kids.

I wouldn't be able to hurt anyone there, but I think of my life without my friends or Aiden and the thought of dying here doesn't seem so bad to me. I would gladly give my life, even if their feelings for me are not true, I know in my heart it's the right thing to do.

My father looks out over the mass of people. We slowly make our way down into the valley, where they all wait for us, a smile never leaving his lips. His confidence despite how outnumbered we are shakes me. All six of our team members are at the front. I lock my gaze with theirs and don't see what I thought I would.

"Give Bree back to us!" Roxy calls out angrily.

"We will call this all off and let chya all go, here and now, if ya turn away and leave Bree," Metikye calls after.

Roxy gives me a soft look that says 'you're going to be all right,' with a loving smile, and I know as I look down the line at my friends that they feel the same. They're here to save me. A tear trickles down my cheek and they all look at me with love.

"Ya didn't think we would give up on ya did ya?" Metikye yells out to me with a wink.

I smile as Roxy nods to me.

"Yeah, not gonna happen girl!" she follows up with.

My tears fall even more. I look all over but I can't see Aiden anywhere. A booming voice calls out through the valley.

"You will all move and let us pass right now. I know now you don't have it in you to hurt Bree, and if that's the case, then having your prince Aiden about to be judged by the maiden if you interfere will give you even more incentive to let us pass," he says calmly.

"That's a death sentence. He is not even a maiden he will die for sure!" the crowd erupts angrily.

Calmly, my father announces, "Let us pass or Aiden gets judged."

20

The Choice

The angry crowd begrudgingly splits, letting us pass. My father doesn't look at any of them as he walks straight through. Slowly, I pass down the line of my friends, a determination that this is not over gives me hope.

A while later, my father pushes me into the carriage to move through the crowd and the valley quicker. The ride is quiet as we leave them all far behind us. I know they are following. They won't give up that easy, but I hope they're planning something to get Aiden back.

"Why are you doing all this?" I ask, breaking the silence.

"I already told you, this has to be done to put everything as it should be. Bree, I know you don't, but you have to trust me. No one understands, but when you face the maiden you will feel it," he assures me.

Something in me, as strange as it may seem, is pulling me, making it very hard to fight the need to go. I think of all my friends who would rather see magic fall than lose Aiden or me. The thought warms my heart, but makes me fearful for the price they would pay for our lives.

Even if they could save us, the closer I get, the stronger I feel it, the need to see her. My father looks at me with a warm smile on his face.

"You feel it, don't you?"

I nod.

He leans down and places a gentle kiss to my forehead. "I knew you would be the one to understand," he says wrapping an arm around me, as he rests his cheek to the top of my head. The simple act strangely brings me comfort. "We have to put things right, Bree. I know you will be strong enough to face this. All will become clear soon enough," he says attempting to comfort me.

I see the maiden coming into view. The small islands suspended in mid-air, growing larger as we approach. It's then I see the massive drop where the valley ends abruptly. My heart is racing now as we get closer. My father looks down at me, noticing my growing distress as we reach the edge. He gives my shoulder a light squeeze. The ground vanishes beneath us as the valley ends with a sheer drop that looks out to the in-between.

I close my eyes, waiting for the sudden drop, but after a few beats, it doesn't come. I open my eyes slowly and see the whole carriage traveling through the air on a road paved of blue light. I can't help my mouth fall open in awe as we travel in a spiral upwards, going higher and higher, the road sparkling beneath us. The stars in the night sky and the moon high make it a dazzling sight.

"I thought there was no magic here?" I ask.

"No, I said porting magic would not work here, and this road is made by the wise ones. Very few know how to use it."

The road ends at the massive island that holds the giant maiden statue. At her feet is a massive platform, where I see my uncle with a blade to Aiden's throat, and ropes of blue light binding him.

"Let him go!" I shriek, launching myself from the carriage towards Aiden.

"NO!" Aiden bellows.

I freeze as my uncle pushes the dagger to stop him from talking.

"Come, Bree," my father says behind me.

He rests his hand at the small of my back to guide me toward them. Aiden is trying to shake his head despite his situation. I stop.

"Release him and I'll do as you ask. Please, just let him go," I beg.

"I'm sorry, my dear Bree, but without him, I can't be sure you will do what needs to be done, and I can't guarantee the others won't come to stop us," he states firmly.

"Can you blame them? This is their lives we are talking about," I retort trying to reason with him.

"Bree, you don't know what you are talking about. Everything is wrong! You are here to make it right," my father says trying to assure me.

"You keep saying that. What does it even mean!? What ever happened to the power to rid magic so only light magic remains?" I ask, desperately trying to find sense amongst all of this madness.

"Bree, step forward and see for yourself. The prophecy is not as they were told. The maiden will only show one the way. That's why the one has to have the heart of a queen, one that will be strong enough to free her people. This was never about power," he says.

I look at him in shock as I see my uncle do the same.

"You said this would destroy magic!" he yells in fury.

"I said magic would disappear and I only told you what you needed to know to get her here," my father says harshly.

"You lied to me, to all of us!" he spits, tightening the ropes on Aiden.

"No!" I scream as Aiden struggles for breath.

"Well, if that is the case, then I guess you don't need this anymore." He releases Aiden from the dagger and pushes his body towards the platform.

Logan leaps through the air out of nowhere, a gust of wind carrying him over the platform, pushing Aiden back to safety. My uncle howls as a lasso of flames wraps around his wrist, pulling him backward, stopping his attack toward Aiden and Logan.

My uncle brandishes his dagger, flinging blades of light at Metikye, cutting at his right upper thigh, and arm.

"Ahh!" Metikye yelps, his lasso disappearing from my uncle's wrist.

He grabs for his wound. He turns his attention back to Aiden, throwing his dagger the same way he did to kill my mother.

"Aiden!" I scream, diving toward him.

Logan knocks past me, diving at my uncle. Logan throws a gust of wind to the dagger, trying to knock it from its trajectory, but only manages to slow it down. Logan struggles to hold it as Aiden grabs for the staff Roxy throws to him.

"Thank you, Rox!" he calls to her.

"Enough pleasantries, deal with this ass, then the niceties," she replies.

Aiden and Roxy fight back-to-back as everyone else joins the battle breaking out all around us. I look up to see dozens of Oregrin's above us bringing even more to the fight. Aiden and Roxy combine attacks, sending a man flying to the maiden's feet, bursting to dust on contact with the platform. Logan has the dagger at a stop now, both men caught in a battle of strength.

An elbow jabs me in the gut. I double over, gasping for breath. A set of arms reach around me, pulling me away from a rogue fireball. I barely get a chance to see Aiden, when blue light blades cut through the air separating us once again, but it's my uncle's blade that has broken free and flies straight towards me in a flash of blinding light.

An abrupt force throws me to the ground as everyone halts, and silence fills the space. It takes me a few moments before I realize why. I look to the platform floor as I make my way back to my feet.

"Bree, step away we can go home. Just take my hand," Aiden implores me.

I go to take his hand. The maiden's platform glows under my feet, and a loud voice rumbles through the air.

"STOP!" the maiden thunders.

"If you leave you will die, without judgment."

I freeze.

"I am the maiden. You are judged as worthy. Your heart will now be tested," says the maiden.

Confused, I ask, "What do you mean tested?"

"You have three choices; leave and die, take the one you love with you from this world, forever leaving these lands in ruin, or throw your-self to the gates above and have a chance to put things as they were meant to be," the maiden informs.

"Bree, no matter what happens we are here with you. If you go, we will find a way to be with you," Aiden says, trying to reassure me, but the maiden immediately rejects his sentiment.

"No! Bree must go alone. You can only travel with her if she chooses you, and only you, if she rejects judgment, Aiden. For her to pick her friends, and you, she would have to take the test," the maiden says knowingly.

"So, the only way Aiden and I can be together is if I sacrifice this world and all those attached to it?" I ask again.

"No, as I said one way is with Aiden, leaving this world in shambles, or the other is to save these lands" the maiden replies.

"That's not true, Bree! We can find a way. This isn't how this will end!"

I look to Aiden and realize there is only one choice to save them all. A loud groan interrupts my thoughts. I look to the edge of the platform where I see my father dragging himself to the edge. I gasp and move towards him. He holds up a hand to me.

"Stop, you can't move off the platform," he says, pulling himself into a sitting position near me.

I notice the dagger in his chest. "That was the flash of light. You protected me, didn't you?" I begin to sob.

"I would die a thousand times over for you, my sweet girl. I know I have made a lot of mistakes, but I genuinely thought by keeping you away from everything, it would keep you pure of heart, but I know now your heart is pure because of everyone you touch and everything you have done."

I kneel down in front of him as he reaches a hand to caress my cheek. "Stop talking like this is goodbye. We can heal you. Everything will be okay," I sniffle.

He smiles, dropping his hands to the ground to help himself push to his feet with a grunt. He reaches over to hold me in his embrace. My tears begin to fall. I feel him move to step onto the platform. He pulls me to him holding me tighter.

"Things are not always what they seem, my petal. I'll be with you every step of the way." He plants a soft kiss to the top of my head. My heart pulls as a tear falls to my cheek.

His foot touches the platform. His body slowly disintegrates, rolling through my arms and fingers. I fall to my knees, and my tears fall in a flood of emotion. Aiden and my friends edge towards me.

"I wish I could hold you right now," Aiden says with sorrow, reaching his hands out to me.

Slowly, I reach over and link my fingers with his. Looking around at my friends, I notice someone missing.

"Where is Logan?" I ask, still looking for him.

Roxy steps forward with tears rolling down her face. My heart sinks.

"Your uncle disappeared after throwing him over the edge. His magic stopped working once you were on the platform. He is gone, Bree," she says, falling to her knees in a flood of tears.

A soul-shattering scream rips from me, rumbling the platform. Echoing the unbearable pain, I feel. I take one look at Aiden. "You have said it yourself from the beginning, we are meant to protect. I can't lose anyone else. No matter the choice, someone will get hurt. I refuse to lose anyone else I love!" I exclaim.

I pull my hands back from Aiden's, turn, and run to the center of the platform. I hear the yells and pleas from Aiden and my friends. I reach the center and jump. I'm lifted from the ground as light surrounds me, and darkness falls. The maiden's voice rings out.

"The choice has been made."

To be continued....

About the Author
H.L Jones is a mother of three beautiful children and married to the love of her life for 15 years, she has an amazing family and incredible friends. By day she is a community care nurse and by night a new author who delights in writing fantasy romance with a little sizzle.
Find me on
Hljonesauthor@hotmail.com
HL Jones | Facebook
hljonesaurthor.wixsite.com/website